Zainab Kathrada Teen Summer Reading Club book prize

Praise for *Hairstyles of the Damned* by Joe Meno

A selection of the Barnes & Noble Discover Great New Writers Program

"Captures both the sweetness and sting of adolescence with unflinching honesty."
—*Entertainment Weekly*

"Joe Meno writes with the energy, honesty, and emotional impact of the best punk rock. From the opening sentence to the very last word, *Hairstyles of the Damned* held me in his grip."
—Jim DeRogatis, pop music critic, *Chicago Sun-Times*

"The most authentic young voice since J.D. Salinger's Holden Caulfield . . . A darn good book."
—*Daily Southtown*

"Sensitive, well-observed, often laugh-out-loud funny . . . You won't regret a moment of the journey."
—*Chicago Tribune*

"Meno gives his proverbial coming-of-age tale a punk-rock edge, as seventeen-year-old Chicagoan Brian Oswald tries to land his first girlfriend and make it through high school . . . Meno ably explores Brian's emotional uncertainty and his poignant youthful search for meaning . . . His gabby, heartfelt, and utterly believable take on adolescence strikes a winning cord."
—*Publishers Weekly*

"Meno is a romantic at heart. Not the greeting card kind, or the Harlequin paperback version, but the type who thinks, deep down, that things matter, that art can change lives."
—*Elgin Courier News*

"Funny and charming and sad and real. The adults are sparingly yet poignantly drawn, especially the fathers, who slip through without saying much but make a profound impression."
—*Chicago Journal*

"A funny, hard-rocking first-person tale of teenage angst and discovery."
—*Booklist*

"Underneath his angst, Brian, the narrator of *Hairstyles of the Damned*, possesses a disarming sense of compassion which allows him to worm his way into the reader's heart. It is this simple contradiction that makes Meno's portrait of adolescence so convincing: He has dug up and displayed for us the secret paradox of the teenage years, the desire to belong pitted against the need for individuality—a constant clash of hate and love."
—*NewPages.com*

W9-BYF-936

Todd Baxter

JOE MENO is the author of three novels, including *Tender As Hellfire* (St. Martin's, 1999) and the bestseller *Hairstyles of the Damned* (Punk Planet/Akashic, 2004), which was selected for the Barnes & Noble Discover Great New Writers Program and has been translated into German, Italian, and Russian. Meno is the winner of a Nelson Algren Literary Award and is currently a professor of creative writing at Columbia College, Chicago. He is the cofounder of *Sleepwalk* magazine, coeditor of *Bail* magazine, and a columnist for *Punk Planet* magazine. He lives in Chicago.

HOW THE
HULA GIRL
SINGS

JOE MENO

akashic books
new york

Cover design by Pirate Signal International
Cover photo by Todd Baxter

Published by Akashic Books
Originally published in hardcover by ReganBooks/HarperCollins
©2001, 2005 Joe Meno

ISBN-13: 978-1-88451-83-5
ISBN-10: 1-888451-83-1
Library of Congress Control Number: 2005925469
All rights reserved
First Akashic printing
Printed in Canada

Grateful acknowledgment is made to reprint the following: "Folsom Prison Blues," words and music by John R. Cash. ©1956 (Renewed 1984) by House of Cash, Inc. (BMI)/Administered by Bug Music. All rights reserved. Used by permission.

Akashic Books
PO Box 1456
New York, NY 10009
Akashic7@aol.com
www.akashicbooks.com

In memory of Johnny Cash

I know I had it coming
I know I can't be free
but those people keep moving
and that's what tortures me . . .

—Johnny Cash, "Folsom Prison Blues"

contents

acknowledgments

With gratitude, thanks to:

Koren, my folks and family, Cheeb, Mr. Mark Zambo, Jake, Chad, Jimmy, Erica Lund and Mark Anderson, Texas Dave, Chris Christmas, Rob Robbins, Michelle Mason, Sheryl Johnston, Randy, Gary, Patty, Don, Julie Caffey, Bill Hayashi, Ann, Alex, Melissa, Alicia, Diane, Lot, Renee, Sam Weller, Sam Jemielty, Shelly Ridenouer, Susan, Laurie and fellow artists and dreamers at the New Leaf, Marion, Paul, Rose, Mr. Hubert Selby, Mr. C. Michael Curtis, Mr. Johnny Cash, Mr. Link Wray, Dr. Michael Schnur, Dr. Morales, Cook County Hospital, Columbia College Fiction Writing Department, Todd and Ashley Baxter, the *New City*, especially Elaine, Dan Sinker, and Johnny and Johanna at Akashic.

HOW THE
HULA GIRL
SINGS

ghost town

Out of nowhere, I did what I ought not to. I thought of the girl I loved, waited for my chance, then robbed the liquor store where I worked. I got in my car, sped away, imagining the howl of sirens where no sirens were.

The highway itself was dark as hell and led up to the sky.

There was no room for headlight beams among the silver stars. Cat's eyes. That's how they glowed. Thick gray eaves of fog hung all along. There was no sign of anything around. No sign of providence or luck. It was like some lonesome dream where it's just you and your desire, left out to burn in the dark.

Did you ever watch the sky at night all over a lonely road?

Night can be the emptiest, most hollow thing you might ever feel driving toward your home, at fifty miles an hour, with an open bottle of port and the liquor store's returns for the night and that sweet plastic-faced Virgin Mary staring down at you from her all-fiery position on top of the red vinyl dash. No, there might not be any room for your poor thieving dreams in that incorruptible night, at all.

The Virgin did a little curtsy as I pulled off the highway and straight down La Harpie Road. The black vinyl steering wheel was loose in my greasy hands. My fingers were slick with my own sweat.

I had never stolen, really stolen, before.

I never had the need.

It's strange the things a desperate man will do to keep sane.

It's strange the things a desperate man will do to keep himself from feeling so desperate in the first place. My mouth was full of spit and cheap liquor. It tasted like old steeple dust. Streetlights flashed somewhere up ahead. I could hear the *dtt-dtt-dtttt* stutter of the wheels over the rough pavement, rattling along to the poor mechanisms in my mind. My eyes began to shut. I needed to sleep. A nice soft place to hide. The engine gave a little start. I opened my eyes.

Then this pretty lady walked right in front of the car.

No.

Sweet Jesus, no.

In those still moments, I could see her soft round face; her dress was long and pale blue. Her neck was thin and made her seem about as real as some shadow. Her lips made a little helpless move as the headlights fell across her face.

There wasn't any time to stop.

The wheel went dead right in my hands.

The baby carriage this lady pushed met the cool steely grill and shot straight up into the dark night sky, losing itself among all that pleasant distance and the sparkle of the silver stars. *Good night*, the tiny round wheels seemed to say, as they spun around. *Good night*, like I was falling right into a kind of dream.

Then it was all over. Then it was as good as done.

I fell out of the car and vomited all over my dull black shoes, right before the night moved in straight through my eyes and sore mouth, knocking me down, pulling me along some desperate road out of my body, out of my own unhappy life, and straight up to Pontiac for a three-to-five bid for manslaughter and reckless driving. My old boss at the liquor store was Christian enough not to press charges for robbery, seeing me sunken in the sad state I had fallen.

"The prisoner will be remanded to the State of Illinois Department of Corrections until his sentence has been served or until the courts see fit for his release . . ."

That night played over in my dreams every evening like an awful jukebox song. I would try to fix it all in my head, stopping just a foot or so short, keeping my eyes open long enough to see this poor lady with her baby carriage, her pale skin lit up with fear and the certainty of that unwieldy moment, her brown hair hanging long down her back, the twisted knot at the end somehow sealing all our fates, and me, me, gripping the steering wheel tighter or hitting the brakes sooner. Somehow I would try to trick myself so it didn't happen and that sky never fell apart, but those still seconds always ended the same: the sound of the engine spinning right through my ears, pulling all the blood straight out of my body, and that tiny blue carriage being knocked up into the night, like it was so light and empty and hollow and was being lifted by the invisible hand of Solomon, straight up, disappearing among the brightest of the stars, taking its place in a fixed spot laid out by Jesus or the Virgin or some fleeting angel somewhere above, just before it all faded to black and was done.

No events before that night mattered anymore.

Those dark little moments suddenly held everything.

All the things that would follow would come from that single hopeless second in all of the heartlessness of space and time. All those things would send me straight through my acquaintance with the old state pen and Junior Breen and would forever change the life I would then lead.

old tattoos

They gave me back my full Christian name and my own clothes and three miserable old Viceroy Golds. I had hidden them in the lining of my red suit coat. They were the stalest cigarettes I ever tasted, I swear. There were some little nicotine ghosts with unfiltered moans that drifted up within that smoke because those goddamn cigarettes were so old.

They gave me back my full name and the life I had lost, but still that baby carriage rolled on cold through my head. It rocked and wavered right past me as I wandered out of those penitent iron gates and back to being a sovereign man. I bought myself a vanilla shake at the Dairy Queen right away and sucked it down slow, holding that straw between my teeth until it was all gone and just a cold feeling along my teeth. Then I bought myself a bus ticket for the passenger line home and took a seat up near the front.

That trip home was kind to me as an open wound.

I sat still in my seat, watching this other con I knew, Jimmy Fargo, feeling up his sweaty home-fried girl, undressing her right on the bench in front of me, trying to give her the time right on those awful gray cloth seats. Jimmy Fargo's girl was a plump red-head with a pleasant round face and a white blouse unbuttoned all the way down to show her ample bosom and freckled white flesh.

There was a wave of pure undulation as ol' Jimmy unclasped her bra. It echoed along my mouth and in my own head.

"Hey, now, watch it back there!" the old buzzard of a bus driver shouted over his shoulder. "Or I'll stop in the next town and turn you over to the cops and they'll send you right back to the old pen."

Jimmy snarled a little and nuzzled his sweet's rouge-stained cheek. I wondered if there was something in his thin eyes that gave him away. Something that gave some accurate sign, some portal of his time spent behind locked prison metal doors. I wondered if the same gray halo hung over my own head. Maybe it was his haircut. Trimmed a little too straight. A little too thin above the ears. My own hair was cut in a high and tight pompadour, trimmed expertly by Darcell, the prison's only barber, who would do a real right cutting job on you if you slipped him a generous tip.

Two years and ten months had faded right away like old skin left dead in the sheets. There was nothing in that time that made me think I'd been forgiven. There was nothing that made me think I'd ever be able to breathe without hearing that baby's soft name.

Hyacinth.

Sent straight up to the sky.

Those letters were burned in my mind in a way I could never forget. The way it had always been figured for me, it had only been a matter of time before I ended up in the pen anyway. Looking back, it seemed my whole life kind of led up to that single moment, accidental and horrible as it was.

They let me go and I took a job back in my hometown of La Harpie, Illinois. There were still some folks that had once known my own old man, Rowdy Lemay, as a decent hog farmer and either didn't remember where his son had gone or never knew exactly why they had both left in the first place. In a small town, rumors tended to circulate and die pretty fast. The problem with that was people might forget what horrible thing it was you did but still remembered your name with a kind of undistinguished shame. It's a thing you can see go dark in other people's eyes and faces. It was a thing I'd expected to find in anyone that had once known me back home.

My own mother had split town when I was ten. My old man had moved away after I had been sent to the pen and now lived somewhere south of Minneapolis. There was no pretty gal or weepy-eyed father waiting outside those concrete-and-wire gates for me. I would be going home to a place where none of my own blood was living and where most everyone else disregarded or completely mistrusted me.

That bus had a sugary smell like sleep.

I fought the whole way between unsettling, unwholesome dreams.

I startled myself awake. I wiped my face and looked down at my hands, worn, but well-scrubbed and clean. Everything was fine. Someone mumbling something right in my ear.

"The only thing you're missing there is gasoline," he whispered. This crazy old man beside me gave a little smile. Then he gave a gentle wink. We were already within the city limits. Nearly at the bus station on Trotter Road.

"Do you need any gas?"

This old guy had a dirty red gasoline can sitting in his lap. His eyes were black, his lips were pale. There were flies sticking to his sweat. Beneath the stink of his breath, there was the faintest odor of gasoline rising up from the can that shook in his lap. "This here gas is only five dollars."

"No. No thanks." I smiled. There was always some kind of poor fellow on the bus. Always some sort of stranger or something unsettling like that.

"This is premium gasoline."

I stared out the dirty windows. It was already getting dark. I shook my head, feeling it turn down in my gut.

La Harpie.

A place of a kind of quiet villainy and secret lust. A place where the dirty dreams of every twelve-year-old man-child were visible on the bus station's bathroom walls in hand-scrawled tattoos of ladies with oversized breasts and inappropriate female genitalia, inaccurately portrayed as a singularly dangerous triangle of doom. Those kinds of drawings set me up for a world of confusion.

I stared out the huge glass windshield and frowned.

A pretty girl walked right in front of the bus.

Jesus—no.

The bus heaved to a stop, burning up its brakes, almost running the pretty lady down where she stood, tall upon her cheap high heels. The girl just shook her head and straightened her white blouse. Those breathy pneumatic doors opened with a hush and she climbed on up.

"Nearly ran you down, missy." The gray-toothed bus driver frowned. The pretty lady just gave a little smile.

"Then you might've mussed up my skirt."

The bus driver gave a weak chuckle and took her fare. She held her black suitcase at her side and took a seat across from me.

The girl was really something. A nice toast-and-butter kind of gal. Her eyes were big and brown, her hair was dark black like fine molasses and ran in curls down to her shoulders. Her whole neck was covered in little beads of sweat. There was a tiny white collection of her perspiration along her blouse's thin collar. I could see her delicate white brassiere moving beneath. I could hear her underwear as she crossed her legs.

My god, I hadn't touched a woman in nearly three years. My hands began to tremble. I began to feel like a real stranger, impure and swarthy as hell. The bus shook a little as it moved. This lady just flipped her curly hair over the other shoulder and stared down at her feet. Then she looked up. Then she looked me right in the face.

"I know you, don't I?"

"I don't think so," I grunted. I turned and held my breath and looked straight ahead. My face began to get all red and hot.

"No, I think I know your name," this woman whispered. "Isn't it Luce Lemay?"

"Sure is." I grinned. "How'd you happen to know that?"

"We've met before. My name is Charlene Dulaire."

"I'm sure I would have remembered meeting a pretty lady like you," I whispered.

The lady blushed a little, then stared hard at my face. She looked down at my arms, along the back of my sweaty hands to my wrists.

"I do know you." Her thin black eyelashes fluttered just once. "I know those tattoos."

"Excuse me?"

Her eyes were bright as she ran her fingers over my wrist, up my arm. Her touch was so light, so soft. I felt my stomach curl into a knot. There was a dark black tattoo of a sacred heart burning along my forearm. She smiled.

"You've had those for a while, haven't you?"

"Since I was about sixteen or so."

Her soft face blushed red like two perfectly round apples turning hard on her cheeks.

"You used to make it with my older sister in high school."

"How's that?" I mumbled. My face was creaking with humiliation.

"Ullele. That's my older sister's name. You used to sneak into her bedroom and make it with her on Sunday nights when our parents were at Mass. My Aunt Fiona, remember her, the one who thought she had a bird living in her chest, she just kept getting crazier and crazier, so my folks would go to church every Sunday and light a candle. Then you'd sneak in up the tree and climb in my sister's room. Me and my other sisters used to listen to you doing it through the heating vents."

"Jesus." This girl, Ullele, her eyes were dark and round and brown, her legs were thin and long, but there was some problem with her teeth. There were three or four extra teeth that made her mouth look huge. It was a horrible thing to see that poor girl smile. Her daddy owned a used car lot in town and was known as Milford Dulaire, the Used Car King of the Greater Southern Illinois and Northern Kentucky Area. He was a tall thin man who hated me more than you could ever believe.

"Which sister are you?" I asked.

"The littlest one. I remember my father wanted to murder you. He really did. He told my sister to stay away from your kind. He called you a hood. He said you were born with those tattoos." She looked away, down at her feet. Those big brown eyes got sad. "He shook his head when he heard about you in that trouble a few years ago."

I gave a frown. I felt like I couldn't breathe at all.

"That was a few years ago all right . . ." I said in a kind of sigh. "It was all some kind of accident . . . it was all some kind of mistake I made . . ."

"My older sister cried all night when she heard you'd been sent away. Cried all night and through the better part of a day. Nearly left a running stream in her bed there were so many tears. But that's Ullele for you. She cries sometimes when the sun's too bright. She'll cry in the middle of the day for missing the night." Charlene gave a little smile and stared up into my face.

"Looks like you made it through it okay. I mean to say, you still look good. How long were you in for?"

"Three years," I replied. "Three longest years of my own short life." This pretty girl was so smooth and soft. I wanted to press my fingers along her lips and kiss her chin more than anything. I wanted to feel something good beside my skin. But now she knew. No parole board could make me a different man in any beauty's big brown eyes.

"Did you ever get married to that girl?" Charlene asked.

"Who?" I asked.

"That girl, Dahlia. My older sister hated her. Said she stole you away from her."

"No, that's not true. Ullele and me broke up a long time before. She started dating some guy from Colterville and she didn't miss me at all after that."

"No. She still has a torch for you. All my sisters do."

Charlene's eyelashes fluttered like a summer dream as she crossed her legs. "So did you marry that girl?"

"No," I said, shaking my head. "That was like a bad joke."

The girl twitched her nose.

"Oh, dammit, I have to go."

"You heading on some kind of trip?" I asked.

"Huh?" She looked down at her suitcase like it was the last thing she expected to find in her hand. She gave a little huff and shook her head.

"Where you headin'?" I asked.

"Oh, I'm going back to my parents' home."

She shot up out of her seat and started toward the front of the bus, then turned around and looked back at me. She gave a quiet smile and stared right at me, making the air around my head seem perfumed and sweet. Then her lips parted and the softest words ever spoken came unbuckled from behind her white teeth.

"Welcome home, Luce Lemay," I heard her say and I felt like I was about to faint. Charlene shook her head and walked to the front as the bus rolled to a stop. The doors opened with a hush. She stepped off and out into the road before I could find a single word to speak. The bus took off again and I felt my tongue come undone from its knot.

"Hey . . . wait," I kind of mumbled. I imagined her young lips firm against mine. I fell back into my seat like an invalid.

"Hey, that sure is a nice suit," the crazy old man beside me said. I nodded. The bus rumbled along, stinking with all our sweat. "That sure is nice."

"Thanks."

"Where'd you get a nice suit like that?"

"I'm not sure."

The suit I was wearing was red polyester, with a red collar, the only suit I owned, the one I had worn to trial, the one that had sat in a drawer somewhere in the Illinois Department of Corrections for three years. It was old and wrinkled and stank of a short stay of incarceration.

"So you want this gasoline or not?"

"Sure. All I got is three dollars," I said.

"Fine, that's fine."

I dug into my suit pocket and handed him three bucks. At the next stop he hopped off the bus and slipped into the Five-Spot Bar on the corner. The bus pulled away just as the old man was probably ordering a strong bourbon in a dirty white glass.

The gas can beside me shook as the bus pulled away.

I leaned back in the seat and stared outside, then dug into the pocket of my suit and pulled out Junior Breen's old letter.

> *To my good old pal,*
>
> *How is life? I hope this letter finds you well and in good spirits. I hope everything is dandy as a peach.*

Junior Breen was one of the few friends I had made in the pen. Junior had gotten out a few months ahead of me. He had gone to La Harpie and gotten a job at a service station there because the owner was an acquaintance of my old man and had a soft spot for cons. Junior got me a room at the old hotel where he was staying. He had been too afraid to go back to his own town. He didn't want to face the things he had done in everyone's shallow stare. He had a kind of face that let you know he was all alone. He was a square guy, but a little strange. I met Junior when he was sitting alone in the library, the only part of the pen that was always air-conditioned, a big behemoth of a man staring hard at one of the glossy concrete walls, mumbling words quietly to himself. His hair was short and brown. He had enormous pork-chop sideburns. His forehead sloped down over his two deep blue eyes. He was carving something with the end of a pen hard into a linoleum desk. From where I sat all I could read were the words *old red organ*. Then he got up all of a sudden and took a seat beside me and smiled, looking me hard in the face.

"Tell you what I miss the most." He frowned. "Ice cream. There ain't nothing like a good ice cream on a hot day like this."

"That's the truth." I smiled. "I'd pay a year of my life right now for a visit to Dairy Queen."

"Name's Junior Breen," he said. He offered me a big white hand. His fist seemed to envelop mine as he gave a hearty handshake.

"Luce Lemay," I replied. "How long you in for?"

"Twenty-five years, no parole." He frowned.

"How many you got left?"

"This is my last one." He smiled.

"Boy, that's swell. Where you hail from?" I asked.

"Colterville. Home of the best Dairy Queen I've ever known."

"Colterville? They do have the best Dairy Queen in the state. I'm from La Harpie myself. Never had a ice cream store in our town.

We used to have to drive over to your Colterville if we wanted something cool to eat."

"Don't know what I'd do myself." Junior frowned. "I'd consider moving, I guess."

"Man, I'll tell you, when I was about eighteen or so I was in love with this girl that worked at that Dairy Queen in your town. She was something. Luanne Wurley, that was her name. You know her? She was something. A real sight. With her little cutoff jeans and ponytail and vanilla shake, she had everything. Used to sneak dillybars to me for free."

Junior kept smiling and let go of my hand. "That sure sounds nice."

"Give a year of my life for a kiss from a girl like that," I said.

"I'd give a year just for the ice cream."

I took to him right away. He was a big man, about twenty years older than me, somewhere around forty-five. He was in for murder of the first degree. He had strangled a fourteen-year-old girl when he was only seventeen himself and left the body out on a plank of wood and sent it down a river. Junior told the jury he thought he was doing the girl a favor. They sent him away for twenty-five years without the hope of an early parole. They thought Junior was something like a mental defective. Don't get me wrong, he wasn't slow, he'd just have these spells where he'd climb into his bunk and sit and stare at the wall for hours. He wasn't dangerous or anything. In fact, he seemed downright scared most of the time. He knew he had done an awful thing and you could almost hear it there, burning in his heart late at night, poor old lug. Junior was a big man. He weighed close to 280. Big and burly but tender as a pup. He was the kind of big guy other cons used in order to make themselves look brave or tough.

"Hey there, fat boy." A con named Toreador grinned. He was in for three counts of theft and one for aggravated assault. He had robbed a carful of old-folks and stolen all their cash and clothes. The cops had picked Toreador up wearing one of the old men's flowered shirts. "How's breakfast, fat-ass? You get enough?"

Junior shoved another spoonful of oatmeal in his big round mouth. Toreador took a seat beside him and put his arm around the bigger man's shoulder. Toreador wasn't that big himself, he was thin and wiry, but his face looked mean as hell, long and greasy, his skin brown and full of pockmarks. "How come you eat so much, fat boy?"

Junior just gave a shrug with his shoulders and tried to finish his grub.

"You like to look so fat? Have big fat titties for yourself?"

"Why don't you leave him alone?" I said. I held my fork in my hand. I could see the thick blue vein where Toreador's blood ran up to his evil head.

"I was talking to fat-ass, if you don't mind?" Toreador turned back and leaned in close to Junior. "So you like to be fat? A big boy like you could be a real wild fuck for a lonely con. I oughta sell you as my bitch."

"Just leave him alone," I said again.

"Hey, I said I wasn't talking to you, OK? If you want to get your ass beat, then keep on interrupting."

Junior's big face was caked with sweat. He was trembling like a big baby. He couldn't move. His wide forehead dribbled perspiration around his tiny doughy eyes. Some spit was bubbling along his mouth. Some snot was flagging in his nose.

"Is he your bitch?" Toreador smiled. "You like those fat-boy titties, don't you? You like fucking that lard-ass, huh?"

"The only cocksucker at this table is you," I said.

"La Santa Angel de la Guarda," Toreador whistled. "You sure have a mouth for such a pretty thing. Make your move, go ahead, pretty thing. Show me what a tough girl you are. Go ahead. Make your move."

I gritted my teeth together hard and flung my metal tray across the table straight into Toreador's chest. Grits and meal flew all over his prison-issued white T-shirt and dirty blue pants. Before I could make another move, he was already at my throat. He had his long thin fingers gripping me tight, choking me hard, banging my face against the cold metal table. *Crack.* I could hear the skin along my nose tear open. Then my jawbone. *Crrrrrrrack.* He began screaming and just kept smashing my face against the table's end. I could hear some correctional officers hollering.

There was my stop.

I opened my eyes and slipped the letter back inside my suit coat. The gas can in the seat beside me rattled with a little song.

I pulled my things together and rose to my feet.

I left the gas can on the seat beside me and crept past the empty benches toward the front of the bus.

The door made a little hush as I stepped out. I was sure of it now. Nothing in that long lonely night seemed like it would ever change. I fumbled through my suit and walked straight into the dark.

honeymoon veil

An angel of lust spoke coldly:

"Lonely tonight?"

Even in a small town like La Harpie there were ladies of the night. Bus and train stations were where they flourished, I guess. They'd pick up men stopping in town for the night or husbands who had just seen off their wives. This girl was desperate, wide-toothed, pale, with a long jagged scar, waiting all alone.

"Bet a lonely ol' jailbird like you wouldn't mind a little company for the night."

I just kept on walking, trying not to breathe in her perfume. Because then it would be over. Then the rest of my seventeen bucks in singles would be spent in lust and I'd be without food or a room. Morning would come and I'd see her sore face, without any of the thousand layers of makeup, then she'd tell me it was time to go and I'd feel worse off than if I had just spent the night alone.

"So how long were you in?" she asked.

"Almost three years."

"And your girlfriend didn't pick you up to welcome you home?"

"Don't have a girl."

"That's a shame, good-looking boy like you."

I just kept on walking. I didn't want to stop. But this pale prostitute kept up with me like we had been walking together all our lives.

"'Cause, I'll tell you, this town ain't exactly kind to strangers. I'm just telling you as a little warning."

"Thanks."

The girl was maybe about seventeen. There was a long gray scar that hooked around from one eye to the corner of her lip. It looked like it had been carved deep by a straight razor. I could smell her sweat. I could smell her perfume, probably just some soap. I needed a woman.

I took a deep breath. I lit a cigarette and exhaled through my nose. The prostitute winked at me and patted me on the shoulder. I fingered a cigarette out of the pack and handed it to her.

"Do you wanna get a room then?" she asked. "We could do whatever you like."

"Whatever I like?" I asked.

"Sure, baby, sure, whatever you like."

"Could I go up to that hotel room and take off all your clothes?"

"Sure you could, sweetie. That's usually part of the deal."

"No, no, I mean, could I go up to that hotel room and undress you slow, so slow, piece by piece, right on down to your last little panty ho, then maybe wrap you up in a nice white towel and slip you into a warm little bath, a warm little soapy bubble bath, and wash your hair for you, then maybe soap up your back and your legs and your face and rinse you off clean, then dry you off nice and good and tie a soft white robe around your waist and kiss all your skin from your sweet little forehead down to your bare white toes? Then maybe tune the radio to a nice country station and wait for a sweet ballad by Tammy Wynette or Johnny Cash and kiss on you some more and more and maybe dance together without any of our clothes and then fall asleep together so tight they think we might have died right there? Could I do that? Could I do that for only seventeen dollars tonight?"

The prostitute's face was all pale.

"You don't want me dirtying up that kind of pretty dream."

She flicked her cigarette into the dark, then turned down the street alone, biting her thin yellow hair. I watched as her shadow grew and then disappeared. I took a deep breath and turned around.

There were small green squares of lawn in front of each house and some gray trees that made a little shade. There were the railroad tracks that stretched out in the distance beside brown telephone poles, all of them curving along the horizon. It was a good dare to get someone dumb to walk along the train tracks right before a train passed by. Nobody I knew got hurt doing it, but it seemed kind of dumb anyway. There it was. La Harpie. A town. Not much to look at, I guess. There was something underneath it all, though. Something like blood or gold. Something small that might fit in your pocket. Like lung cancer or a lucky dime.

I walked a block to the St. Francis Hotel, where Junior Breen had a room. It was red brick with a black metal fence. Three floors and a patch of lawn with dark black stains of mud.

The streetlamps suddenly flickered on.

It was just beginning to get dark. Welcome home, Luce Lemay, on the worst night of your life. You lousy hayseed. I coughed a little, then opened the front gate with a squeak and walked up to the front door. I pressed the door buzzer that was hanging out by its yellow and red and blue wires.

Bzzzzzzzz.

Old Lady St. Francis answered the door. Lord. Her eye shadow was a purple nightmare that ran all over her forehead. Her breath poured through the screen door. She had a can of beer in one hand

and a lit Marlboro in the other. She was a short, mean-faced woman with a poof of gray hair and huge flabby arms. After her husband shot her lover dead and then turned the gun on himself, she lost her mind. She thought she was St. Francis of Assisi. She laid the dead to rest right under her back porch.

"Do you have a room to let?" I asked.

"You know someone here?"

"Sure, sure. Junior Breen. He said I could find a room here."

"He did, huh?"

"My name's Luce Lemay. I talked to you before. I just got out."

"Out? Out of where?"

"Pontiac. I'm on parole."

"Another jailbird, huh?" she grunted. "You from town here?"

"Just outside of town, ma'am."

"Hayseed, huh? Grew up on a farm?"

"Yes, ma'am. Hog farm."

"Well, I thought you were here about the cat."

"Nope."

"Because it's too late."

"Too late? What's wrong with the cat?" I asked.

"It's dead."

"Huh." I let out a little sigh. "So do you have a room?"

"You heard me the first time."

Old Lady St. Francis didn't make a move. She just stood there and took a sip of beer, clinking her yellow teeth on the can.

"You gonna let me in?" I asked.

"Why? What the hell are ya up to? No-good bums coming in and out of the jailhouse . . . It's a hundred fifty a month. How much you got now?"

"Seventeen bucks." I frowned. I pulled the money out of my pocket and handed her the cash.

"That'll do for the next few days. You getting a job or you all planning a heist?"

"I got a job lined up at a service station, same as Junior."

"Lucky enough someone pays that fathead at all. A fathead and a hayseed. I don't see how that station will stay in business."

"I dunno, ma'am."

Her deep bloodshot eyes moved over my face. She took a swig from the silver can and unlocked the door.

"Junior's in his room. You can have the one next to his. Third floor all the way down to your left." She dug into her pocket and handed me a key. "Thieves and liars, the lot of you!"

I took my chances and walked inside. There was a huge wooden staircase that rose in the middle of the building up to the other floors. There in the lobby was a tiny white cat all laid out on an old white sheet, lying there dead on a glass table, surrounded by white candles, wearing a red crocheted dress, in some sort of funeral. It lay there on its back, its head dropped to one side. Its two tiny front paws were bent down like it was begging one last time. I stared at that cat for a minute, then walked right through that awful front room and up the stairs to the third floor.

There were old paintings of different saints being massacred or put to death. Saint Bartholemew with hot arrows in his throat. Joan of Arc tied to a fiery stake. There were tiny dead birds hanging all along the walls, all wearing pink crocheted sweaters.

I walked down to the end of the hall. There was the last door. I patted down my hair in the back. The door was painted black, open a little. I took a breath and knocked a few times, holding my brown bag of clothing. That's all I had, a brown bag full of underwear, a few socks, some pants and some T-shirts, the red suit I had on. My whole life fit in a garbage bag. Already I had a plan, though. Get a room for a while, get a job, save up some money, buy a car, and head out to Hollywood. Maybe work at a gas station out there. Fall in love with a movie queen and spend the rest of my days by the pool. Maybe just work at a service station. You know they have to have them. Tinseltown. I had no real idea why I wanted to go out there. Maybe it was just a dream I had overheard in prison or on that crowded bus while I was asleep.

I gave a gentle knock.

"For God's sake, go away!" Junior hollered from behind the door. "Just leave me alone!"

I pushed open the door a little more and stepped inside. "Junior?" I whispered.

Big ol' Junior was curled up in a fleshy ball behind the door. There was a wad of snot hanging from his nose. His eyes were puffy and red and full of tears. He looked like a lost little kid.

"Jesus, pal, what's the matter?" I asked.

There, carved into the wood floor by Junior's big white hands, was a single darkly lettered word.

Perfidy.

Junior heaved himself to his feet. He gave me a big hug, nearly lifting me up off the red carpet floor.

"You made it. You made it OK."

"Sure I did, pal. What's the matter with you?"

"Strange things have been happening, ol' pal. Strange things." His round face got all serious and grave. "Been hearing things in my closet all week."

"Things in your closet?" I smiled.

"Then I heard Toreador got paroled and I thought he'd catch up with you and put a bullet in your back before you ever made it here."

"Paroled . . . but . . . I thought he had been transferred . . . I thought he was gone."

"Guy Gladly told me last week. He said it was good as a done deal."

"Maybe he still thinks I'm in the joint."

"Sure, sure, pal, you're probably right. You know I'm just out of sorts when it comes to those kind of things. Sure."

Junior gave me another monstrous hug.

"It's good to see you, pal. I'm sure we've got a mighty bit to talk about." He grinned.

"This landlady is crazy, huh?" I asked.

"She's the one giving me all them nightmares at night. All her dead animals all over the place. Got me thinking there's ghosts hiding in my bureau and under my bunk."

"Guess I'll take a look at my room then."

"She said you could have the one next door."

I stepped out into the dark hallway and slid the key into the doorknob. The door creaked open a little as I stepped inside.

The Virgin Mary frowned right at me, holding her lips together in the saddest smile I'd ever seen.

"What is that?" I mumbled.

There was a huge painting of the Virgin hanging along the wall. She stood in sweet white and blue robes, with her hands clasped above her red sacred heart, as the flames of perdition burned around her, surrounding her in a red-orange glow. Her skin seemed so pale and soft. It really was the saddest, most real looking painting I had ever seen. It was lit by the light from the streetlamps outside. From the draft along the thin wood walls, its canvas flickered like she was taking a little breath.

"What is this?" I asked.

Junior flicked the light on.

There was a long parade of the dead running from that lost little room. The room itself was really some kind of storage closet, about five-by-eight. There were crickets and pale-winged moths scattered everywhere, all over the walls and ceiling, these crickets, hundreds of them, chirping. There were about thirty thin cigar boxes—Te Amo, Royale, Havana Maduro—all different-colored boxes lying on a little white bed. Caskets. Caskets for the dead. All these boxes were filled with tiny dead animals, all white and browned skeletons rattling in their empty tombs. There were all kinds of other unfortunates left in several little piles along the floor. All kinds of other little birds and squirrels and chipmunks and even a tiny tabby kitten lay still and dead and in the open without proper burial arrangements. This room was a kind of warm, stuffy nightmare, some sort of shrine to little dead things everywhere.

"My god," I muttered, closing one of the yellow cigar boxes. "Jesus, what is all this?"

"St. Francis has been busy lately, I guess," Junior mumbled. His eyes widened a little like he was walking in a dream.

"But where the hell did she get all these dead things?"

"I think she's been going around the neighborhood late at night and doin' them in herself. There's no way there's this many a dead animal lying around town."

I kind of smiled as Junior grabbed a stack of tiny cardboard caskets. He slung them under his arm as all the bugs scattered and flew about. He dropped a few to the ground. Thin yellow skeletons full of gray hair and feathers spilled on out, disappearing into the darkness under the bed.

"Sorry 'bout that." Junior said. He gently pushed the remains all into one box and shoved it under his arm. "We can go bring these downstairs." He nodded, dragging the dead out.

It was all right. It was a place to sleep. Just for a few months. Maybe even a few weeks. At least I had good company. I thought about Junior and smiled. I didn't feel like such a hood around him. Maybe that's why people have friends at all. Not because they like them so much but because they don't make them feel so much worse.

The both of us took a seat on my bed when we were done relocating the deceased.

"Me, I'm kind of wondering how the ladies in town are looking since I've been gone," I said.

"They're all pretty as can be." Junior grinned.

"You make it with any yet?" I asked.

"Not just yet."

"Know any we can call on at least?"

"I know this one place. It's not too far away. Guy Gladly told me where it is. I can spot you some money if you need it."

"Just until I start getting paid."

"That's a square deal to me. Ol' Guy said these girls were all clean and pretty. Don't mind if a feller was a con or not, just as long as he has some manners about the whole thing."

"That sounds fine to me." I smiled. "We're probably the best-behaved convicts the state of Illinois has ever released."

The dark in this motel room was perfumed and sweet.

The windows were open. The purple drapes were slapping against the sill, *slap-slap-slap*, taking a real beating. I took a seat on the red heart-shaped bed. It rocked a little with my own weight. I unscrewed the metal cap from the cheap bottle of wine and took a slug. My heart was pounding right in my throat. I felt fit to burst.

The old telephone rang.

Rrrring.

I let it go.

Rrrring.

Be quiet, telephone.

Rrrring.

"Hello?"

The black phone fit right beside my ear. There was someone's red lipstick on the mouthpiece.

There was no one on the line.

"Hello?" I whispered again. "Anyone there?"

"The Savior's already on his way."

"What?"

"The Lord told me to call you tonight and let you know He's on his way. Prepare your soul! Repent and rise from your wicked state!"

The plastic handset turned cold in my hand.

"Who is this?" I asked. Then the line went dead. I put the phone back in its cradle and took a long swig from the ol' apple wine. Maybe this was a dumb idea after all. This crazy Toreador was out on the streets. Maybe he was already following me. And the police. I didn't need to run into them ever again. Maybe it was all poorly planned. My hands were aching and sore. I stared at my pants, then gave in and unbuckled them and undid the zipper quick.

A fragrance of cold rose petals and copper. Like flowers in your bloody throat.

I turned and faced the open door. A pretty girl was just standing there smoking. Cool and pale and tall and blond. All the blood left my mouth and drew down to my thighs.

"The door was open." She smiled. "Hope I didn't startle you."

"I was . . . just having a kind of daydream," I mumbled.

"Too many dreams during the day will keep you awake at night." This lady shut the door and locked it twice.

"Don't think I ever heard that one."

"You paid the man in the lobby, right?"

I nodded.

This pale lady slipped off her black shoes. One, two. Beautiful. There were her bare feet on the red carpet floor. Bare digits. Bare toes. I kept looking at the shimmer and shine of her red-painted nails. My god, I felt ready to burst. The soft white skin just below the firm knob of the ankle moved as she moved. "Come to me, sweetie," she whispered.

This lady pulled her white sweater over her head and sat down on the bed.

"What's your name?" I asked.

"Ms. Bunny." She smiled. Ms. Bunny; I grinned. The thin black brassiere on her chest looked like a special invitation to a dream. *Hello*, it said. *Come cling to me.*

This lady stood and wrapped her arms around my head. Then we began to kiss. All I could feel was her mouth. All I could breathe was her lips. It was heaven. A heavenly kind of prostitutional kiss.

"You from town?" Ms. Bunny asked, as I buried my face in her chest.

"Yep."

We began to kiss again.

"You done time in the pen?"

"Yep."

Those lips were stuck right outside my teeth as she began to talk once more.

"My brother's up in Joliet right now for five-to-ten."

"Huh."

I fought to unsnap her brassiere. I was not much in a conversational mood. I began kissing her long white arm, inch by magnificent inch.

"My brother stole a car and some hi-fi stereos," she said.

"Uh-huh."

This pale lady looked at me and blushed, then gave a little nod. Her short blond hair shifted over her face.

"Sorry, sometimes I tend to talk too much."

"It's OK. I don't mind. Reminds me of every other girl I've ever been with."

"All of your girlfriends been chatty, huh?"

"Yep. I don't mind. Makes me feel like I've known you then."

Ms. Bunny took off her black panties and switched off the light. In the dark her legs were crossed together tight like long slender headlight beams. Then I could see her bare thighs moving apart. There was a flash of her bare skin as she slipped beneath the cool white sheets. I took off my pants and laid beside her, then began breathing heavy in her ear.

"You ever make it with a professional before?" Ms. Bunny asked.

"Just once." I kissed her neck. "When I was sixteen."

"Sixteen? That's awful young."

"My uncle came into town on my birthday and took me to a motel like this."

"Were you nervous?" she asked.

"A little, I guess."

"Did they treat you OK?"

"Sure. Didn't last that long, though. Felt like they should have given me half of what we paid back, but that lady said the sexiest thing I ever heard a woman say."

"What was that?"

I sat up in the bed and stared through the dark at her smooth round face.

"Why you wanna know?" I asked.

"Tricks of the trade and all that." This lady, Ms. Bunny, ran her hand up and down my chest.

"You really wanna know, huh?" I asked.

"I sure do."

"Well, this lady just laid on her bed all naked and just looked at me and said . . . '*Take me.*'"

"'Take me'?" Ms. Bunny gave a real sweet high-pitched giggle. "That was it?"

"That was it." I frowned.

"That's all she said?" Her blue eyes were wide with disbelief.

"Doesn't sound that sexy now, I guess."

This lady began kissing my neck, still laughing. I could feel her body moving underneath my chest. Her skin was smooth and supple and soft. Her legs were long and thin and held me to her tight. She dug into her purse for a condom and fit it on me in place. Then we began making it, kissing each other long and soft. Then she fit her hand into my hand and held her lips right beside my ear and made a whisper like a little song.

"*Take me.*"

I pressed my hands against the inside of her thighs and felt my way in and started doing my thing, holding my mouth right outside her ear as she put on a real floor show, moaning and cheering me on, until I was done and shivered hard and fell asleep quick like a baby in her long white arms.

There, in between those smooth white sheets, I had myself an awful dream that ran loose through my poor old skull.

This tiny blue baby carriage rolled right toward my head.

Maybe it was coming to pick me right up and take me off to some other sad sort of dream. I couldn't really tell.

I was thrown right out of that dream about a half hour later by the sounds of the walls shouting out loud.

"Get the hell out of here, you jackass!!" some lady screamed. "Go on, get the hell out!!"

I sat up in the bed and listened hard over Ms. Bunny's wheezy breath.

"You crazy nut, go on, get out!!"

I pulled my pants up and unlocked the motel door. There was Junior, half naked, trying to button up his drawers, standing in the dark like he was ready to cry. The rest of his clothes were being thrown at him through the adjacent open motel room door. Junior looked up at me sadly and shook his head. This red-headed hooker in black negligee threw his big black shoe hard and hit him in his chest.

"Hey, what's all this yelling about?" I asked.

"Your friend here is some sort of funny guy," the red-haired hooker snarled. "Some sort of weirdo or something."

"What? What the hell do you mean?"

"He asked me to tie the sheets around my head like a wedding veil."

"What?" I mumbled.

"He asked me to tie the sheets on me like a wedding veil, like we were getting married."

Junior just stared down at his big white bare feet, holding back his big silver tears.

"First he sits on the bed for half an hour without saying a goddamn thing. Then I get up to leave and he asks me to dress up in the sheets like a goddamn bride. Boy, your friend here has a real sorry sense of humor, I'll tell you. What is he, a goddamn comedian or something?" She had her hands on her thin hips and was smoking a long brown cigarette like some sort of dragon.

"Just leave him alone." I bent over to pick up one of his shoes. "You got your money, right? Just keep your damn mouth closed." I patted Junior on the back and handed him his shirt.

We walked back in the dark all the way to the Old Lady St. Francis Hotel without saying a word. We marched up the big black stairs and down the dark red hall and outside our separate doors, and then Junior lifted his head and shrugged a little and turned to me.

"Sorry 'bout causing all that trouble. Guess that girl musta misheard me."

"Ladies of her profession can sure be awful." I smiled.

"I guess." He let out a big sigh and shrugged his shoulders again. "Long as you had a good time, I don't feel like it was much of a waste."

"Well, if it makes you feel good, I had a fine time myself."

"That's good all right."

"Good night then, pal." I nodded.

"Good night." Junior frowned.

I unlocked my door and began to step inside.

"Luce?" he asked.

"Yeah?"

"Mind if I sleep on your floor tonight?"

"What's that?" I said.

"I got a full day of work tomorrow and I wanna be sure I can get some rest. I can't sleep in my own room feeling low like this." There was a tiny sparkle of hope in his big blue eyes.

"Guess if you don't mind the floor," I said.

"No, I don't. Not at all."

He unlocked his door and got his pillows and blanket and spread them out on my tiny floor. I got undressed and laid in bed and listened to him begin to fall asleep. I could hear him tossing and turning against the grain of the wood.

There was a thin white light that broke from between the floorboards and shone right through. There was a quiet moving sound like bare feet creeping over the thick wood. I sat up in bed and looked around. There was nothing there. The door was closed and locked. The Virgin Mary breathed slowly as the draft pushed against her soft canvas skin. I looked around again. It sounded like someone small was keeping very still in that awful old room. Making enough noise just to let itself be heard. I laid back down in that bed and tried to keep my eyes shut and closed tight. There was something moving in that dark room, I was sure. It sounded like a baby carriage creaking along my spine.

"No angels, no angels in this here room," I heard Junior whisper in his sleep. I leaned over my bed and stared at his face. His eyes were closed tight, his hands knitted as he gave a few more whimpers and finally fell into a lumbering sleep. It was a pleasant, sad kind of hummingbird little snore he whispered that made me feel right at home. It made me glad I was splitting that tiny room with some other con, hearing him fight through his nightmares and weighty guilt. It made me glad I wasn't spending the night all by myself alone.

two birds and one broken wing

"A bird crawled beside my head in the middle of the night."

Me, I was still asleep.

"A tiny bird."

There was a tiny baby bird resting in Junior's big white hand. He was sitting on my floor, holding that bird so gentle and tight. "Found it sleeping right beside my head."

"Christ." I frowned, wiping the sleep out of my eyes. "A bird was sleeping beside your head?"

"Sure was. Found it resting beside my ear." He uncupped his big hands a little, showing the tiny bird. It made a little peep, nestling against Junior's thumb. Its black eyes flickered open and closed as if it had just awakened from a sound little sleep.

"There are more of them boxes under the bed," Junior mumbled. "There's a whole nest under there."

"Jesus."

"Must've creeped on out," Junior said.

"Must have."

"Must have crawled on out and been living under the bed," Junior stated.

"That's what I'd guess, too."

Junior rubbed his big white thumb along the bird's soft black side.

"Can you tell what's wrong with it?" I asked.

"Maybe a broken wing. That's what I think anyway."

"Guess you can give it to the Saint downstairs to take care of." I frowned.

"Yeah, if I wanted it to end up tacked to the wall wearing a sweater."

"Huh," I said. "Maybe you can turn it loose."

"No, no, this bird is sick. Can't even fly. Wouldn't last a night in the outside world. And it's got the smell of human on it."

"Smell of human?" I asked.

"Sure, sure, if the other birds smell it, they'll peck it right to ribbons. It ain't fair this thing got its wing broken. No, I think I'll make a splint for it and keep it in my room till it looks a little better."

"If that's what you think." I smiled.

"We better get up moving for work."

"What time is it?" I asked.

"Five-thirty."

"Christ." I laid back down in the bed, then sat up again. Junior got up off the wood floor and opened my door and stepped out into the hall.

"Whatcha got there, slim?" a cold voice whispered. It was L.B. from across the hall. Another con. He had served five years for robbing a truck-stop diner and an eighteen wheeler. When L.B. was finally apprehended, the owner of the tractor trailer visited him in court and knocked out seven of his teeth with the end of his boot before three or four bailiffs could keep the truck driver at bay. "Is that a wee little bird?"

"Found it beside my head," Junior mumbled, staring into its tiny black eyes.

"Looks like a wee little songbird. Is that what it is?"

I stepped out into the hall and looked this other con over. He was short but thick, like a wrestler. His skin was pink and his hair was blond but shaved off. He had big nostrils that flared hard as he breathed. He had a pack of smokes rolled up in his left sleeve and the shiniest, whitest teeth I had ever seen.

"Who the hell are you?" he asked me.

"Luce Lemay," I grunted.

"You the one that ran down that baby, I heard."

I nodded just once, then looked down at my feet.

"I did five in the pen for unarmed robbery myself. Nearly got away but I forgot to take off the goddamn air brakes."

"Huh."

"I heard you was from town."

"Not exactly. Grew up out on a hog farm."

"Hayseed, huh?" L.B. snorted. He kept giggling like he was having the goddamn time of his life.

"So whatcha plan on doing with that bird there, Junior?" he asked.

"Make a splint for it."

"A splint? What the hell good's that gonna do? You already got your goddamn hands all over it, slim. No other birds are gonna wanna go near that thing. That one's good as dead. Bird with a broken wing oughta be killed."

Junior shook his head and unlocked his room. He stepped inside quickly and slammed the door closed.

"Big dumb fool," L.B. sniveled. He unrolled his package of smokes from his sleeve, then fingered one on out. "Care for a smoke?"

"Not at all."

He ran his tongue over his smooth white teeth. The two front ones popped right out onto his tongue. They glimmered and shone smooth and hard.

"Goddamn." He frowned, digging his fingers inside his mouth. "These buggers keep falling out."

"You get them made for you in the pen?" In the pen nearly everyone had bad teeth. Teeth that were as forlorn as their owners' lives. It was an easy sign to see who was a lifer or repeat offender by looking at their teeth. If you were pretty young, pretty new, that is, your teeth would be in a sad state of dental hygiene. If you stayed in prison long enough, you might be lucky enough to receive a whole row of shiny new teeth. It appeared to me this L.B. must have spent some considerable time behind bars to have such a perfect smile like that. "So they give 'em to you in the pen?" I asked again.

"Hell no. Grinded 'em down myself." L.B. grinned.

"Yourself?"

"They ain't nothing but driveway gravel. I used a file to shave 'em into shape." He held one of the teeth between his thumb and forefinger. It was smooth and shiny like a work of art.

"How do they keep from falling out?" I asked.

"Little bit of spit and denture grip does the trick." He plugged the two gravel teeth back into place and spat a silver droplet of drool on the floor. "How's all your teeth?" he asked me, moving his face closer to my mouth.

"They're all fine. Thanks for looking anyways."

I stepped back inside my room and closed the door tight. The Virgin Mary breathed a soft red breath to herself as I got dressed for my first day of work. A dirty white T-shirt and a pair of blue pants.

I met Junior outside the hotel. I sat on the front stairs and smoked a good-morning cigarette until he came out. Boy, he was all decked out in dark blue slacks and a dark blue shirt that had his name embroidered in nice white letters. He was all cleaned up and looked straight and good.

"That bird'll be OK all alone by itself, don't you think?"

"Think it'll be just fine," I said.

"I left my door open and told L.B. to check on it sometime today."

"You trust that feller going in your room?"

"There ain't nothing in there to steal. Besides, I'm just looking for any reason I can to bust out his awful teeth."

I laughed and lit up another cigarette and watched Junior comb his hair up into a greasy pompadour that he checked in a car's side mirror.

We walked the half-mile to the Gas-N-Go and stepped inside, with Junior mumbling about the bird.

"Maybe I'll get that thing a nice cage."

The Gas-N-Go filling station was a gray-white building that rose like a short little chapel, coming to an arch with its thin black roof. There was a time when I was a kid and loved the strong-sweet smell of gasoline so much that I'd gotten myself into trouble starting small backyard fires, mostly lighting up dead birds and soda pop cans. That's the first thing that hit me about the place. That sweet-strong smell of old summer days lighting fires in the dirt.

"This here second chance is only worth a damn if you take to using it right."

Clutch Everest was the owner of the Gas-N-Go and the nicest goddamn man I had ever met. Both his arms were covered in faded black jailhouse tattoos; a skull, a swallow, a grass-skirted hula girl. He was an old black-haired con who had served time for lighting his ex-wife's house on fire in the middle of the night, burning her and her new husband up pretty bad. He said he had no remorse about the whole thing. The pen had made him a man and had introduced him to Jesus Christ and the fundamental nature of the second chance.

"At first, when I burned down Delilah's house, I used to think of myself as dead. When they pulled that girl and her new beau out all burned up red and black, well, I thought I was dead right there. Left my goddamn soul buried under that heap of ash. I began living my life without direction or hope. Then, after a few months in the pen, I properly met Jesus Christ and straightened out my life good."

"Huh." I nodded. Junior Breen, Clutch, and me all stood behind the white counter, facing the double doors. The windows of the service station shone with the glimmer of the rising sun, moving over all our faces. I looked around a little as Clutch spoke. There were three short rows of a variety of sundries and snacks, bags of chips and cookies, soda crackers and motor oil and the like. The last aisle faced a length of glass-door coolers that chilled some soda and juice and beer. There was an old microwave near the counter in front and a rusty coffee machine beside it, dripping the morning's first brew. The sun had just begun to peek through the top of the glass, shining right into my eyes. It felt good moving over my face, all that warmth and sun made me feel good to be out of the pen and still alive.

"The Scriptures told me all about different kinds of saints that had taken to ill-begotten ways and led various lives of sin, but then they called on the Lord Jesus' name and found themselves clean and saved. I figured if it worked for Saint Paul or Saint Teresa, all those words might have some meaning for me."

"That's great."

"Hell, son, I can tell I'm boring you, but this is all for your own good. You're out of the pen now and have a free life and it's easy for a man of your own special kind of moral quality to fall back into his old ways. Your father was a good ol' pal of mine. I guess, for his sake, I just don't want to see you heading back up to Pontiac for another sentence anytime soon."

"Thanks," I said. "Means a lot."

"It oughta. I'm trusting you and Junior to be honest and hard-working, and if even for a minute I have a sneaking suspicion you're ripping me off or slacking or ain't flying straight, I'll fire you so fast your blessed young head'll spin like a top."

"I understand."

He offered me a hand to shake. "Good. Let's get to working then."

That day Clutch showed me the ropes. He walked me through ringing someone up on the register, how to turn the pumps on and off, what shut-off switch to throw in case of some emergency, what kind of thieving to watch out for, who should and shouldn't get the bathroom key, and which nudie magazines he favored to read. Junior watched and nodded and smiled and winked at me, patting me on the back after I rang up my first customer all right.

"This boy is smarter than a whip," Junior smiled. "You'll have no problems from him, Clutch."

"I hope not. I'm trusting you two can be responsible enough to take care of this place in a few weeks all by yourselves."

Toward the end of the day, right around about six o'clock, while Junior was out front sweeping around the pumps and ol' Clutch was in back going over the previous day's receipts, a little towheaded boy came in.

"May I have the bathroom key?" the boy asked. He had short blond hair cut into an uneven buzz, and some dirty blue jeans on with muddied knees. His sneakers were untied and caked in mud. There was a nice red scab just beginning to peel along his chin, the fault of those untied shoelaces, no doubt.

"Sure you can have the key. Keep it clean."

"Sure will." The boy smiled up at me, then disappeared right behind the last aisle. When he came out of the latrine, he fidgeted with something in his hands, then stopped and moved whatever it was around inside his pocket again, then dropped the silver bathroom key on the counter and started on out. The boy's little round face had been bright and red and covered in sweat. He had nearly run right out the front doors, nervous and suspicious, holding in his breath.

"Hold it right there," I said. "Whatcha just stuck in your pocket back there?"

There was a small but ominous bulge in the pocket of his blue jeans. Just the right size for some candy or cookie.

"Empty out that pocket, son."

"No, sir," the boy snarled. His greasy little blue eyes were determined and round.

"What's your name, boy?" I asked.

"Monte Slates," he muttered, digging his hands into his pockets tight.

"Well, listen, Monte Slates, unless you want me to call your parents and the police on down here for lifting candy bars or cookies or whatever it is, I recommend you empty out your pockets and show me what you're hiding in your hand."

The boy's face was red.

"I'd really rather not, sir," Monte whispered, scared as hell. He stood before the counter, completely still, holding his hand inside the back pocket tight as he could.

"Well, I'd really rather you did."

"Do I got any other choice in this matter myself?" he asked.

"None that I can see. Unless you turn over whatever it is you got hidden away, I'm gonna have to go in the back there and tell my boss I caught a shoplifter. And believe me, my boss is meaner than hell when it comes to someone stealing."

"Christ," this kid, Monte, frowned, "I don't wanna go through that."

"No, I guess you don't."

Monte shrugged his shoulders and pulled his fist out of his pocket, then opened up his hand. There was a silver foil-packaged condom smuggled tight in his palm.

"How old are you, boy?" I asked.

"Eight," he mumbled. "And nearly a half."

"Nearly a half, huh? What's a boy your age need a thing like that for, son?"

"Make the best water balloons." Monte frowned. "Throw 'em off the top of the underpass down at the cars."

"Huh. I see. I guess I did a bit of that recklessness myself when I was about your age," I whispered to myself. "You get this out of the machine back there?"

"Yes, sir. For two quarters."

"Well, why don't you just go on and buy a bag of balloons for a dollar somewhere instead of wasting your money on those?"

"The lady at the dime store knows me and won't sell balloons to me anymore 'cause she caught me throwing water bombs at her car."

"That wasn't too lucky, was it?" I grinned a little, then handed the kid back his prize. "Make sure you don't hit any squad cars. I hear the sheriff doesn't have much of a sense of humor here."

He took the condom and put it in his back pocket and shot out the door. Junior came in and looked back over his shoulder as the boy ran off and disappeared around the front of the pumps. Junior walked up to the counter with a smile and a confused look.

"What was that all about?" he asked.

"I just had a conversation with myself from twenty years ago."

Junior just blinked and turned the Marlboro sign on the door over to "Closed." Clutch appeared from the back room and wiped his eyes. He looked all worn out.

"You boys did good work today. Go ahead and take yourselves a six-pack home."

"Thanks, Clutch." Junior winked at me and pulled a silver six-pack from the cooler. We each had two before we even made it back to the street that led to the St. Francis Hotel. Just as we turned the corner to our block, a squad car came up and pulled beside us along the curb.

"Good evening, fellas," Sheriff Dwight Fontane said with a smile. I froze. Junior just shrugged his shoulders and took a swig of his beer. Sheriff Fontane slipped the car into park and hopped on out, tugging his gun belt around his waist. His face was sharp and square and came to a flat edge with his cinder-block chin. He was a little overweight, with bright eyes and a happy smile.

"Whatcha boys got there?" the sheriff asked. "My, I'd love one of those about now."

Junior smiled, taking another swig. "Care for some?"

The sheriff twitched his black mustache once, then shook his head. "I better not. It's an election year."

Junior relaxed, patting me on the back.

The sheriff stepped up to Junior, sticking his hand out to shake. "Dwight Fontane, good to know you."

"Likewise," Junior said

"You boys just been released?" the sheriff asked. "You're working already?"

"At the Gas-N-Go, down the road."

He smiled. "That's good to hear. Already back on the straight and narrow." He looked me in the face, then frowned sadly. "You're Luce Lemay?" he asked. "It's been three years already?"

I shook my head. "I'm out on parole."

"Parole, huh? Well, glad to see you're back among your own people."

I stared down at my feet. "Yes, sir, we aim to make the best of our situation," I said, not too convincingly.

"Who's your parole officer?"

"Man named Blakes over in Colterville."

"Talked to him yet?" the sheriff asked.

"Not yet."

"He's nice enough. Kind of busy all the time, I guess. Not like me," he said with a grin. "Well, I've taken enough of your time. Just stopped you to say, well, I guess my wife was the one who suggested I let you know we're praying for you."

"Thanks," I said, still staring at my feet.

"Guess I should be working," he said, climbing back into his squad car. He gave the car a start, grinding the engine hard. "Shoot, already started." He smiled to himself, then pulled away, and we watched as he disappeared from view, both of us surprised by the welcoming.

We marched on up to the third floor and Junior stopped suddenly outside his door.

"Christ. I forgot all about that poor bird." His face looked serious and grave. He slid his key into the lock and gave it a turn. He pushed the door open, holding his breath in tight, listening for that baby bird's little chirp. There was no sound. No sound at all. He stepped inside his room slowly, then became perfectly still.

"No," he kind of whimpered. "He wouldn't do something like that."

I looked around Junior's big square shoulder and shook my head. There, lying on the floor, with a long dark nail pounded through its throat, was that little baby bird.

"He wouldn't," Junior snarled. "He just wouldn't."

That baby bird just laid there completely still, held in place by the black nail which had been driven through its little neck. The evening light broke right through the window, casting the bird's black shadow along the floor.

"Jesus Christ," I mumbled.

"That ain't right," Junior whispered. "That just isn't right at all."

He turned around, walking past me, and strode across the hall. He laid his big fist against L.B.'s door in a heavy, thunderous knock. L.B. opened his door quick, grinning with the most wicked smile I'd ever seen.

"Got you some kind of problem there, Junior?" L.B. chortled. "Looks like you got something on your mind."

"Nothing at all," Junior smiled. Then he sucked in a breath and curled up his fingers into a big fist and slammed that bastard L.B. hard across his grinning mouth. *Crack*. Junior swung again, this time smacking that bastard's short, protruding nose. A thick line of blood dribbled around L.B.'s mouth. Junior grabbed the smaller man around the neck and began slamming his fist into the side of L.B.'s head.

"All right, Junior, all right," I said. But he didn't hear a word. He grabbed L.B. around the collar of his shirt and flung him hard against the wall, sending him straight into a hanging mirror that shattered all across the back of L.B.'s head. L.B. sunk to the floor, covering his face, swearing and cussing and kicking at the air around him. There were little shards of mirror that twinkled all along his pink skin, shining bright over the tiny scratches and his swollen, bleeding nose.

"Motherfucker . . ." L.B. mumbled. "Stupid motherfucker. You pushed that too far," he whispered. "Done push me too far."

Junior just stood over that poor fool, tensing his fingers into hard white fists that were smeared with L.B.'s blood and snot, squeezing his fingers together hard. He gripped L.B. around his throat and pushed him up against the wall, then dug his big white fingers inside L.B.'s mouth. He yanked out his polished-white teeth and held them tight in his trembling hand.

"This is the end of it now, you hear? We're all evened up now.

Don't even think of trying to settle things any different. We're all even now, you hear? Don't try anything dumb or you'll never get these teeth back."

L.B. nodded as his face began to turn white. He ran his pink tongue over the hollow spot where his teeth had just been. He spat a little in some defiance, then wiped his lips with the back of his hand.

"They're gonna know. This whole town'll know what you did."

Junior shoved L.B. once more, then strode out of the room. I stood there with a frown, staring at L.B.

"What you looking at?" he finally grunted, swiping at the air. "What's so goddamn funny there, con?"

His empty gums gave a little whistle as he spoke.

"Nothing. Nothing at all." I closed L.B.'s door for him and went across the hall. Junior had already pulled the bird free from the floor and had it cupped in his white, quivering hands.

"Best thing I can do is bury him outside, I guess." He stroked its thin belly, holding it tight in his hands. Its dull eyes were half opened, slightly covered by thin pink eyelids.

"Do you need any help with it?" I asked, patting him on the shoulder.

"Naw, I'll do it alone." He pulled a silver can of beer free from the plastic six-pack ring and walked out of his room. The dark black nail still lay on the floor. I bent over and picked it up, then held it in my hand. I looked up. Hung right on the opposite side of my wall was another picture of the Virgin Mary. This one was of her holding the Baby Jesus in her arms, cradling him under her blue veils. Her skin looked so soft and warm and blushed. There was a gold halo all around her head, wrapping the Baby Jesus in precious holy light. I stared at it for a long time, holding my breath to watch as her skin seemed to almost be trembling, almost

sighing as she rocked her baby to sleep. I felt myself grow quiet
and still and calm, just staring into her sweet pleasant face. Then
I heard some kids shout something somewhere outside, playing
some game, and I turned and looked away. I snatched the last can
of beer from the plastic ring, closed Junior's door, and walked
down the huge hallway stairs and out to the backyard.

Junior was right beneath the white wood porch, sipping his
beer and digging in the soft black dirt. That precious little piece of
land had to be the most fertile tract in all of the Midwest. There
was enough bodies laid in that little square patch to grow a few
dozen acres of corn. I crept under the porch and knelt beside ol'
Junior, sipping at my beer as I watched him prepare the bird's
resting place. He had a shiny gold-and-yellow cigar box and a thin
little tissue to serve as a burial cloth, I guess. He held the tiny bird
in his hands, rubbing his thumb over its side.

"That little thing had the nicest little eyes I've ever seen," he
whispered, slow and quiet like he was a little drunk.

"Sure did." I smiled. Then I looked down at the dead baby
bird and sucked in my breath quick. Its tiny black eyes were both
gone. They had been plucked out. There were two tiny black holes
in the sides of its soft little head. It was awful seeing a baby bird
all mangled up like that.

"L.B. did this to that bird? Tore out its eyes?"

Junior shook his head, still holding that poor bird tight.

"No. Just stabbed its neck."

"Then what the hell happened to its eyes?"

"Took them out myself just now."

My teeth shook in my head. I looked Junior hard in his big
round face. His eyes were black and solid and firm. I took a swig
of beer and looked away.

"What the hell didja do that for?"

Junior mumbled something I couldn't quite hear. He laid the

tiny bird in the yellow cigar box and gently pulled a tissue over its body. He dug into his front pocket and placed L.B.'s three teeth around the bird's head like a kind of crown. Then he carefully closed the top and fitted the box into the hole he had dug. He knelt beside it, staring down at the yellow tomb, moving his hand over the lid, gentle and slow.

"Why did you pluck out its eyes?" I asked again.

"To keep those pretty things from being eaten out. Pretty little bird eyes shouldn't be eaten by the worms."

"Well, where did you put them?"

"Didn't put them anyplace yet."

I shuddered a little and wondered exactly where they were right then.

He nodded to himself, then began pushing the dirt over the top of the box in delicate little waves of black earth.

"There, that's good." Junior frowned. He wrote a single word lightly in the dirt, right over its grave. *Hush*. Then he took a long sip of his beer, clearing his dry throat. We both crawled out from under the porch. Junior stood up and wiped off his hands on his pants, then finished off his beer and crushed the dull silver can in his hand. The sun had just set. Rays of light still broke from the clouds. He looked like a giant standing there, but innocent and young, too, staring up into the sky, searching for the first star of the night. He mumbled something to himself, raised his hand up close to his eye, and pinched a silver star between his thumb and first finger, then closed his fingers tight and shoved that star he caught in his pocket right quick. We both took a seat on the steps of the back porch and stared down at our feet.

"Christ, Junior, you sure are a strange fucker sometimes."

I took a slug of beer and shook my head with a grin. Junior gave a little smile, then patted me on the back hard.

"Don't have to tell me twice. Heard it all my life."

a beautiful thing

No restless heart beats still and red and alone for long.

A kind of undeniable love began to blossom at the old Gas-N-Go. Junior started leaving messages for some secret love in black plastic movable letters on the sign out front. It was his duty to change the sign every week. It all started simple at first, maybe even as some kind of mistake.

> *Motor oil sale—2 for $3*
> *The Special: Spark—you ought to have*

Poor Junior had solely misplaced the word "plugs" from "spark," but in that sweet sentence there began appearing some kind of mysterious confession on that rickety white sign that hung out there alone in the sky.

> *Super sale on all used tires*
> *Fair and round as*
> *beguild eyes sapp'd*
> *w luv*

No one said a thing at first. Not even Clutch, our boss. Maybe he thought it was kind of a sweet thing, Junior having a crush on some lady. Maybe he thought ol' Junior deserved love just as much as anyone. So our gentle-hearted patron just read the sign like everybody else, whispering to himself who he thought the object of Junior's cryptic missives surely was. But no one had a clue. Those messages were as confusing and hard to discern as any love signal I'd ever been sent.

Special—headlite bulbs
Alite thru th dark et nite
to tarry safely pure

Nearly everyone that entered the gas station would come up to me or Junior and shake their heads with a certain amount of curiosity and frustration.

"Sure is a peculiar sign out there." Some old man wearing big blue overalls and a red baseball hat frowned. "What's that last part mean?"

"Don't have a clue myself." I smiled. "Junior here is the one that arranges the signs."

Junior just shrugged his big shoulders and finished sweeping up the floor.

"What the hell does that sign out there mean?" the old man mumbled, shaking his head hard.

"It's awful hard to see at night." Junior frowned, sweeping under the rack of candy and gum. "It's a lot easier when you have working lights."

"What kind of nonsense is that?" the old man asked.

I just shrugged my shoulders and rang him up for a soda pop and twelve dollars of gas. It didn't bother me that I didn't understand. I could see Junior was a quiet kind of man, a man who liked to keep the sweetest, most private things to himself. He liked to

keep most of his life locked away tight in that big barrel chest and
only let it shine out through his eyes once in a while.

Soon enough, those messages out on that sign began attract-
ing a lot of curious kinds of customers. Soon enough, whenever
I'd look out those front windows there would almost always be
someone driving by in their pickup or car slowing down enough
to read the message fast, then they'd always shake their heads to
themselves when they'd realize they couldn't make any sense of it.
People would drive by every Saturday afternoon when Junior
would change the sign and try to sound the messages out as he
made them, reaching up all alone on that ladder with his box full
of black plastic letters.

Milk—1.12 a gal
cool n pale
as a vestal breth
from petal'd lips

By then, Junior and I began having separate shifts. He'd work
the morning, from six until two, then I'd come in at two and work
until ten. I kind of enjoyed working late at first. I could sleep in
until nearly afternoon, lie in my bed most of the morning, smoking or reading or dreaming, or take a walk around town down to
the Boneyard River, or buy myself new shoes or clothes, and still
have time to eat lunch and then go off to work. But then it slowly
began to get to me. Sitting in that gas station all alone. Nothing
but the music of crickets chirping outside to keep me company.
Nothing but the darkness of night moving quietly by my side. I
spent most of my time looking out, up into the sky through those
gray front windows, all covered in creepy-crawling insects,
scratching at the white light inside. I'd sit there at the Gas-N-Go
all alone, singing some honky-tonk songs to myself, something

maybe by Carl Perkins or the King, straining my voice under those dull blue fluorescent lights, staring out through the big, dirty-gray windows, watching people fill up their lonely tanks with gasoline and leave their money with me and disappear back into the dark from where they came. These homely, milky-faced housewives with bubble-headed babies strapped to their yellow housecoats and hips who pumped gas into their long brown station wagons, or old leathery-mouthed hog men with big tan Stetson hats who wiped their pickups' windshields free of dried bugs, or the young, sweaty-foreheaded farm boys in blue flannel who had borrowed their older brothers' green-striped El Caminos, all souped up with chrome and silver that gleamed and streamed, they all gripped those long silver handles and slid the nozzles in and stared up into the dull blue night with the cool urgency that there was indeed some kind of destiny. That night, that sky, that whole universe seemed to be in constant motion, spinning in strange orbits of circumstance above my head, but not me. Not me. Me, I was stuck, as I ever was, in the pen or at that job, it was just the same. Watching the whole world gas up and go could leave a fella feeling awfully trapped and awfully lonely, if you can see what I mean.

After work one night, I had enough, finally.

I locked up the register, switched off the pumps, made a drop into the safe, gave the floors a quick sweep, and made sure the front glass doors were locked. I just started walking then, with nowhere to go particularly. Not that I'd admit anyway. But I had been thinking of the spot all night, there was one place on my mind. I followed Junior's sign straight to a solemn bedroom window through the rural dark. I stood outside that girl, Charlene's, parents' house, running my hand along their white picket fence, sweating and mumbling to myself. Their house was nice and white and big. Their yard was green and long and wide and had thick weeping willow trees planted all around. Their green eaves hung on down, slumbering and whispering so gently in the dark. I hopped over the wood fence and crept along through the soft shadows cast down by those sleeping trees, holding my breath in tight, wiping the sweat and grief out of my eyes with the back of my work shirt sleeve. There was a light on in one of the windows on that second floor. I knew it right away. Her sister Ullele's bedroom. I had crept through the same dark the same way nearly a hundred years before. I felt out of balance all of a sudden. I hid behind a willow and took a breath. I felt like I ought to turn around. I had no idea why I was there. I looked up into that lofty bedroom again. There was the light in the window all right. There was some shadow still moving inside.

I was like some kind of teenage boy all over again. I rubbed the sweat from the palms of my hands onto my black work pants. I tried to hold in all my breath and hope and panic all at once, looking up into that shining white light, praying to see poor Charlene's golden face and some of the sweetest, most unconsenting brown eyes I'd ever seen. I climbed the thick, rubbery willow tree, digging my hands along its thin limbs, climbing up its tallest green branch. Then I shimmied out to the glowing bedroom window, nearly entirely out of breath. I knocked against the shiny pane just once, right before I got afraid that this wasn't Charlene's house or bedroom window at all. I could almost see some greasy-faced machinist waking up and returning my knock with the business end of a loaded shotgun. I shook my head and began to crawl back down the tree. Just then the window shade parted a little, and the darkest, most pleasant brown eyes appeared, squinting right into mine. It was Charlene. No other lady I had ever met seemed so beautiful and detached. No other woman seemed so lovely and mean all at the same time.

"Get down out of my father's tree." She frowned. Her hair

glistened light brown from the light cast over her bare white shoulder. She had on a thin white slip that barely covered her most soft, most sighing parts.

"This isn't your father's tree. It's its own tree. I'm just borrowing it for a while tonight."

"That's the silliest thing I ever heard. What are doing staring in my window at this time of night?"

"Hoping I could talk to you, I guess."

She shook her head, giving a little frown. "Listen, are you gonna get down? I have to go to sleep. I have to work in the morning."

"Where is it you work?" I asked.

"If I tell you, will you leave?"

"I guess. If that's what you'd like."

"I'd like to go to sleep."

"Well, I'd like you to kiss me."

"There's not much of a chance of that." Her eyes seemed so brown and deep all of a sudden. "If I tell you where I work, will you just leave me alone?"

"OK, sweet pea."

Charlene furrowed her thin black eyebrows right at me.

"I work at the Starlite Diner. Down the street."

I smiled, feeling my teeth fill up my face.

"That's only two blocks away from where I work."

"Where's that?" she asked.

"The Gas-N-Go."

"I should have known."

"Oh, don't be like that." I smiled. "I happen to know you're a little sweet on me."

"Not in the least. Besides, I could never bear to associate with such trash." She smiled a little, leaning over the window pane. I could feel the heat from her white skin moving over my face. "Now, will you kindly remove yourself from my father's tree?"

"For a kiss?"

"No."

I shrugged my shoulders a little.

"I guess I'm just gonna have to start singing then."

Charlene shook her head. "My father might still be awake. He already hates you for driving my older sister mad."

"Mad?" I mumbled.

"Lovesick." She sighed, fluttering her thick black eyelashes. "He had to buy her a brand-new pony when you stopped coming by. Then the pony got sick and died and my father found Ullele sleeping out beside it in the barn, broken up and crying your name. Then she was never the same since."

My face felt cold. I shook my head. "That was ten years ago."

"So? He still had to buy her that pony and we all had to listen to her crying all the time. It was a horrible thing you did to her. Making her sad like that. I would push you right out of that tree if I had the nerve."

"You're just afraid to kiss me."

"Is that so?" she asked.

"Afraid I might drive you mad."

"Not in the least." Charlene sighed, tossing her curly brown hair over her shoulder.

"Then why don't you give me one just to find out?"

"Nice try."

"So are you gonna let me take you out one night or not?" I asked.

"The night hell freezes over."

"Could take a long time." I frowned. "Be an awful shame not to go out just once to see if your sister was right."

"Did you know I talked to her today?" she asked.

"Huh?"

"I told her you were back in town. She didn't say a thing about it. She's up in the asylum in Lademe now. Doesn't make sense of too many things."

"Lademe?" I mumbled. There was an asylum up in Lademe where they sent you after you completely went out of your mind. I had known a convict at Pontiac that had spent some time there. He said they wouldn't let him sleep. There was always someone shouting or crying or screaming like mad.

"Yes. It happened about a year ago. She had moved in with this man from Colterville who used to tie her up and lock her in the closet when he would go on off to work. She tried to get away but he kept sweet-talking her on back, and it all finally ended when she tied him to the bed while he was asleep and turned on the gas and left him there to be poisoned all alone in the middle of the night. But he woke up and started screaming for help and the police arrived and there was a little hearing and then they decided poor Ullele needed to take a quiet little trip."

My face felt like it was bright red. I had no idea what to say. I felt like it was all somehow my fault.

"That's awful," I said quietly.

"It is. She's been up there eight months now. Doesn't seem to be doing her much good."

"Why'd you tell me this?" I asked, not looking at her sweet round face.

"Thought you might wanna know. She was your girlfriend for a while, right? She lost her virginity to you and all." She frowned, running her finger right past my hands along the thick brown branch.

"Is that what she told you?"

"Yes, she sure did. She had said you two were planning on getting married and all."

"Christ!" I shouted. "That's the worst lie I ever heard. Your sister lost her virginity a long time before me somewhere in someone else's backseat."

"Is that so? So I guess my sister is a liar, huh?" Her eyes flashed up, right into mine, full of anger and fire. I felt my chest and stomach tighten hard. I wanted to reach through the window and kiss her right there.

"So I'm supposed to believe you over my own sister? I think I should push you right off that branch for being so smug, don't you?" Right there she could have asked any question and I would have said, "Yes." She kind of flipped some of her curly brown hair over her shoulder and held her mouth closed.

"Are you gonna give me a kiss or not?" I asked.

"Not in a million years."

"Fine." I gave right in. I shook my head and began to climb down the tree.

"Where are you going?" she asked. The strap of her slip alighted from her shoulder down across the top of her arm. I could almost see the roundness of her smooth white breast.

"I'm going home."

"Home? I didn't think you'd just leave like that."

"I'm sick of being called a hood. Good night."

"Well, fine. Fine."

"Fine," I repeated, leaping off a lower branch down into the soft green grass.

"Fine!" Charlene shouted, slamming her window closed. That cool lush electrical light flickered off and left me standing alone in the dark by myself.

"FINE!!!" I shouted as loud as I could, then hopped over her parents' lousy picket fence. "Always thought you were kind of a scrawny girl anyway! You old maid!"

I walked down the dark desolate street, still mumbling things to myself. Two cold headlight beams stopped right upon my face. A big red pickup truck pulled to a halt beside me. I could hear a gravelly voice over the rumble of the engine as it idled in park.

"You Luce Lemay, right?"

I nodded once, squinting hard to see who was behind the wheel. It was a dark face. I felt my innards turn cold. I felt like I was about to be shot down. The red door swung open. I saw someone's white fist a few seconds before I felt the blow across my teeth.

"Stay the hell away from my girl!" he shouted. My head snapped back as the bastard swung again, cracking me hard in the jaw. *Snap!* I felt one of my back teeth roll up against my tongue like a tiny stone, dangling by a thin red string.

"Girl?" I mumbled, spitting out blood. "I don't know no one's girl."

He cracked me in the mouth again. This time the loose tooth shot right out and did a little dance in blood as it hit the paved ground. I looked up at his face. It was big and white and square-shaped. There was a huge white scar just above his lip that still had a few stitches of thread left in the skin. His hair was reddish-brown and kind of black along the crown where it rose in twelve hundred greasy cowlicks.

"My name's Earl Peet. Charlene's my fiancée, you understand? A no-good like you crawling all over her makes me sick. Stay the hell away from her, you understand?"

Somehow this big juggernaut had his thick hands wrapped around my throat. Somehow I couldn't throw a punch to save my life. It had been that girl. She had made me soft in the head. Earl Peet punched me square in my left eye and shook me again.

"Stay away from Charlene, you understand?!!"

"But she didn't mention anything about being engaged."

"Well, that girl doesn't know what she wants right now. I don't need you fouling things up between us."

He squeezed my neck with his fat thick fingers, nearly making me choke. "Just stay the hell away." He pushed me into an old brown sticker bush and I landed on my head in the dirt. I could hear him step back into his truck, shift the engine into first, and pull away before the ringing arrived somewhere in my ears.

I fell into my bed that night still dreaming of her face, hoping she'd somehow be standing over me when I could open my left eye right.

No lonely old swollen eye or broken tooth could persuade a cruel mistress like Fate. I made no mistake with Earl's unkind threats. But I ran into Charlene again just by chance. Just by luck Junior and I happened to stop by the Starlite Diner the next night after work.

"Do you know there's something mysterious in that little shake of yours? Put a spell on a lonely man." This square-faced trucker sweet-talked Charlene from his booth, scratching his red beard as it ran wild across his wide face.

"Rivals the mysterious bits of food left in your beard, I dare say." Charlene smiled. This girl's face was round and soft and mean whenever she spoke. Her hair was so curly and brown and shined and moved. Her hair smelled like a peach, like summer, like tender fruit. Charlene was tall and thin and wore this cute frilly blue-and-white-and-pink waitress uniform that showed off her great legs. Being honest here, when Junior and I walked through the silver doors, I couldn't take my unloyal eyes off her. The way she moved, her shoulders were small and kind of hunched over a little as she carried a big order of burgers and coffees to a silver-trimmed table. She had a tiny run in her nude-colored stockings that shot up from her ankle to the middle of her thigh. I couldn't have stopped looking at her to save my life. Her face was all hot from running around. She kind of sighed as me and Junior pushed through the doors. We took a seat at a booth, collapsing right into the red vinyl. Charlene came right up to our table and smiled. Her lips were red and caked hard in lipstick. Maybe she had just put it on. There was a little smudge of red on her white teeth. She came right up to the table and placed some menus in our hands.

"Hello," I mumbled.

"Hello."

Her mouth parted a little. "The soup today is chicken noodle," she said. It sounded like the nicest thing I ever heard someone say. "What happened to your face?" she asked.

"Ran into a doorknob." My left eye was still pretty swollen. My missing tooth had stopped hurting a few hours after it fell out. Now the side of my tongue was cut up from fiddling around with the sharp gap between my teeth.

"Oh? Some doorknob." She leaned the serving tray against her hip and held her breath like she had something to say, but then just shook her head and walked away to take that trucker with the red beard's order. My face was red. I could feel heat coming off my cheeks.

She glanced over her shoulder quickly, maybe to see if I was watching her. I dropped my eyes. Maybe not in time.

Charlene leaned behind the counter on one hand, staring right at me. She blew a big pink bubble of gum. It formed slowly from her lips, then grew and popped. She picked the gum from her mouth and slid it back inside, all while staring right at me.

"What are you doing?" Junior asked. I didn't even know I was standing.

"Making a damn fool out of myself." I shrugged my shoulders and walked up to her. Charlene dropped her eyes and ran her finger along the counter, humming to herself.

"You ready to order?" she asked.

"No, not yet," I answered. "Let me ask you a question. Do you like working in this place?"

Charlene shrugged her shoulders and kept looking down at my hands.

"I don't know. It's OK."

"It seems pretty lousy, that's all," I said. Right after I said it, I realized how awful it sounded. She kind of twisted her eyebrows up and leaned back against the counter. I couldn't smell her hair anymore over the greasy food and cigarettes. I looked over my shoulder, around to that bearded trucker with a red cap and blackened teeth. He kind of curled up his upper lip and choked down another piece of red cherry pie. "This just seems like a crummy place, I mean."

"I don't know," she repeated, looking away. "Did you ever eat here?"

"No . . . Well, once or twice."

"Then how do you know if it's crummy?"

I felt like I had made a mistake. I gave a little cough to cover it up. "That dress sure makes you look funny," I mumbled.

"Is that so?" Her fingers smoothed over the cottony blue material, down to the pink frills. Her legs moved beneath as she shrugged her shoulders again.

"It's just a ugly-looking color is all," I said.

"I don't remember ever asking you." Her mouth was hard and small and round.

"Pink? Pink is a lousy-looking color. Especially with pale legs." I grinned.

Charlene pushed her skirt down and kept her hands over her thighs.

"You are an asshole," she whispered. Her eyes were bright and shiny like she was about to cry. I shrugged my shoulders and kept looking down at my hands.

"Forget it," I murmured. Just for the hell of it, I looked up into her face, right into her eyes. Charlene raised her bare leg and ran it along the back of the other, peering down at the counter as I looked across the dull white linoleum to her hands. They were small and white and plain, no rings, just plain white digits, which looked really nice and clean and pretty. I looked down at her hands, she looked down at her hands, I couldn't look up, I don't know why, I couldn't say a damn thing, all I could think about was her hands, about wanting to hold her hand and take her outside to kiss her, but I was pretty sure there was no way that was going to happen anytime soon, because no one was talking or even breathing now.

"Maybe we could go out . . . when you're done working . . ." I heard myself kind of stammer.

"This is really a bad time. My boss is here. I have to get back to work. You should go."

"Maybe . . ."

Her eyes lifted a little, right into mine. I thought I was going to burst into bloom, like flowers were going to blossom from behind my mouth and eyes, but then Charlene just kind of dashed from the counter and pulled away some dirty dishes and disappeared into the back behind a silver door. Then that was it. That was all. I rubbed the side of my face and then tapped the counter.

"OK, well, it was . . . ahh, nice talkin' to you again," I said to thin air. I turned and fell into the booth beside Junior.

"Did you just ask that girl out?" He smiled.

I nodded just once in reply. "Christ, yeah."

"Well, how did it go?"

"Poorly."

"That's OK, pal." Junior grinned. "There's more than one pretty girl in town. The pretty ones are usually trouble, I've come to learn."

that sweet young bird ain't sweet no more

No dainty gloom could make a body feel more lonesome than missing a tooth. It made me feel improper to smile. Losing that molar over a girl who wouldn't even spare me a kiss made me feel like the imperial king of all fools.

Nothing else could make me feel so low.

Then Dahlia did.

Trouble in a tight white skirt and bargain-basement makeup strode right in. There was a slender silhouette that appeared in front of the glass doors of the Gas-N-Go. The last thing a single man wanted to see. There was her tiny behind bobbing from side to side as she applied her thirty-second coat of red lipstick. I stared out that awful window looking up at Junior's poor sign, trying to look away.

> *Road flares $1.00 ea*
> *rosy n*
> *fulmin-ating*
> *as two cheeks*
> *in folly'd spring*

The glare from Dahlia's purple eye shadow must have stunned

me for a moment, because the next I knew, I could hear the bell above the door give its dull, pallid toll. There was nowhere to go. Dahlia had found me in my worst, most desperate state, missing a tooth and lonely as hell.

"Plum thought I was half mad. Thought you were some kind of oily dream standing there all heavenly like that."

I knew it was her right away. That voice. That undeniable low honey-toned drawl. Dahlia spoke each word in a whisper designed to move any man she wanted inches closer. I don't know if they teach that after you become the head cheerleader in a small town, but it was one of the many attributes that set Dahlia apart from the rest of the girls I had known. Dal had been born a woman and made every boy in her grade crazy until they were old enough to truly understand that an unsatiable belle breathed the same breath as them.

Dahlia stepped right up to the counter and looked straight into my eyes with the biggest, sweetest smile I had ever seen her wear, except when I had asked her to our Junior Promenade, which was, of course, against my will.

"Tell me now, what's a body supposed to do when she finds her one true love's back in town?"

"Christ Jesus," I murmured, staring at the way the light from all the windows burned through her white skirt and showed her fine lines. There were her tight blue panties hidden somewhere beneath. The same blue pair of panties had kept me to Dahlia's side for all of my junior year at La Harpie High and had assuaged me through the Junior Promenade, which had eventually ended with her bare white hips beside mine in a parked car somewhere down her parents' street.

"Luce Lemay, God's insufferable improvement for any of my wildest dreams." Dal glimmered. "How come you don't call me to get yourself off anymore?" Dal hadn't changed in the three years

I'd been away. I had called her a few times from the prison up in Pontiac during the first months, overcome with lust, dying to hear her voice dripping with dirty talk. I would call her up and then she'd say something like, "I have on only a wet white blouse," then I'd nearly faint. Soon enough I found out all the lies she spun around me, and the whole sordid affair made me sick. No man needs a dishonest lover, imprisoned or not.

"How have you been, sweet tart?" Dahlia whispered, leaning way over the counter. Her big white sweater hung way off her bare white shoulder and I could see the fabric of her blue brassiere strap poking out from beneath. "Tell me I'm the most beautiful thing you've ever seen."

"That might not be a lie," I mumbled.

"Good enough for me." She smiled. "How long has it been since you took me in the backseat of a car and made mad passionate love to me?"

I shook my head and looked down at her nimble soft hands.

"Dal, you're wearing a wedding ring," I mumbled. There right on her left ring finger was a huge diamond that sparkled nearly as bright as Dahlia's blue eyes.

"That's right. I'm spoken for now." She sighed. "Missed your one great chance."

"How's that?" I asked.

"You could have had me. Who knows what would have been?"

"So who's the lucky feller?" I asked.

"Favor Muller. Damn near made an honest woman out of me."

"Well, that's sweet. Captain of the football team and head cheerleader getting hitched." Favor Muller was dumb as a rotten log. Much worse off, too. He ran the garbage dump at the end of town. Inherited his fine fortune from his old man. Poor Dal was now the Princess of the Trash Removal Kingdom of La Harpie, Illinois. It seemed like a just post.

"Was only a matter of time before we got together, I guess."
Dal smiled. "I'd still let you take me in the back to show you what
you missed."

"That's awful sweet, Dal."

"Don't know any other way, puddin'. So you're working here
now, huh?" Her eyes sparkled kind of emptily as she looked
around. "You like it here?"

"It's not so bad. Clutch trusts me with the place by myself.
Not too many men would do the same."

Dal blushed a little, then looked away. "So where are you living now? With a friend?"

"I live at the hotel down the street."

"With that crazy old lady? Well, that isn't right. A sugarplum
like you shouldn't have to turn to the pity of strangers."

"I don't mind so much. I've got a pal of mine who lives in the
building. It's not so lonesome since I started working nights."

"Don't you lie to me, Luce. Remember, I know you. You must
be feeling awful living there in that ugly old hotel. Which reminds
me, what happened to your poor face?"

"Fell down a flight of stairs."

"That's not what I heard. I heard you ran right into the end
of Earl Peet's fist. Messing around with his girl."

"We just happen to be old friends," I said.

"That's not what I heard at all. I heard Earl caught you climbing out her bedroom window one night, grinning."

"You know me better than that." I sighed. "I'm not one to
mess with another man's girl."

"That is too bad." Dahlia grinned, running her fingers over
my hand. I smiled, feeling her breath move all across my neck and
face. "Because we could meet sometime. Me and you. You and me.
We could get together and see what there is to see."

I swallowed, forcing all the spit from my lips down my throat.

"Christ, Dal, you sure know how to make a man feel all right. That Favor is a lucky man."

"You don't know the half of it." She frowned, brushing some hair out of her eyes. "Call on me during the day if you ever wanna learn the rest."

Lord.

Dahlia blew me a kiss and shook on out back into the heat. I tried to light a cigarette but my fingers were trembling too much. The square kept slipping out of my hands. This was all from the same woman who had led me to that luckless state. Somehow I was an awful forgiving man where lust was concerned.

The bell above the door gave another ring.

These two young, dirty-faced, round-headed kids kind of weaseled in. They had their hands dug deep into their jeans pockets and their eyes were down at their feet. They crept up to the counter and stared me right in my eye. There was one red-faced kid with freckles and red hair and the other had greasy black hair and pink lips. They looked like they had just got done wrestling with each other in the dirt.

"Gimme a pack of Viceroy Golds," the red-faced kid stammered. I gave a little smile, lifting my head off the counter.

"How old are you, pal?" I asked. He couldn't have been any more than twelve or so. He licked some sweat from his upper lip.

"Eighteen," he lied, digging his fists around in his pockets.

"Eighteen? You got some sort of ID?"

They kind of looked at each other.

"Nope." The freckled kid frowned.

"You're gonna tell me you two are both eighteen?"

They both nodded slowly.

"Can't sell 'em to you boys. Sorry. Wish I could. But I don't wanna lose my job. I happen to know there's a cigarette machine at the diner down the street. Maybe you can scare some up there."

"Thanks a lot, asshole," the little red-faced kid mumbled. Him and his pal walked on out, swinging the door closed without another profane word.

The next day at the gas station, I couldn't get Dahlia out of my head. I straightened out a rack of snack cakes and fruit pies trying to keep my hands busy. A big, wide-faced trucker in a cowboy hat came in to buy three or four nudie magazines and gave me a good wink as I slipped them into a brown paper bag.

"More discreet that way," I mumbled.

"To tell you the truth, son, my wife prefers me reading these nudie books to getting screwed behind her back. Nothing worse than a dishonest spouse, I'll tell you."

I nodded.

"Hell, I knew a man down the way from here, Diamond Lou Feltis, a hog man. He had himself a pretty little wife, few kids, a plot of land, nothing too expensive, but everything was real nice and sweet. Well, this fool took to fooling around with motel whores and then he lost it all for lust. Someone's husband came after him with a shotgun and leveled off his head while he was in bed with some other guy's wife. There was so many pieces of his brain and head and face left stuck in that wall, his sweet wife had them bury a piece of the wall. Saddest thing you ever seen. Burying a yellow-wallpapered part of the wall like that."

I gave a low whistle and shook my head.

"Nearly got killed for the same thing myself. Used to see a lady every Thursday for a drink and some pool and a nice romantic interlude at her house while her husband was at work, and one day he came home and found the bed was unmade and nearly chopped off her damn head with a butcher's knife. Wouldn't have blamed him if he came after me. Don't think there are things worse than cheating on your wife. Not even murder. Hell, if you murder a man, he's dead. Don't feel any more pain. Break some-one's heart, well, that kind of heartache goes a long way. Might as well just shoot 'em dead so they can't feel any more pain. Nothing I can stand worse than a dishonest man."

"Amen to that," I said.

The cowboy patted me on the shoulder, then gave a big, greasy-toothed smile. "I like you all right, boy. Look a little wan-ton, but I can tell you got a good heart. Stay the hell out of unmade beds."

I rang him up for ten gallons of diesel fuel, a bag of corn chips, and three magazines.

The next day, I met with my parole officer, a man named Billy Blakes, from Colterville, who drove on down and had me sign some papers. He was his own little picture of defeat. He was a short, balding man with brown hair and thick glasses, but a thick man, a man who might bust your nose with one stiff blow if prop-erly pissed off. He talked quiet as hell. He gave me a little inter-view, asked me if I had been involved in anything illegal since my release, asked me how I was adjusting, if I needed anything. He didn't seem to have much hope for me, and I sure as hell wasn't a hardened criminal. He had probably seen a thousand cons like me get released, then fall off the straight-and-narrow and end up back in the pen. You couldn't blame ol' Billy. He was working against a thing as undeniable as human nature.

"Please, Luce, if you run into any problems, give me a call. How's the job working out?"

"Fine, Billy, fine," I said.

"OK. And the living situation?"

"Just fine."

"You're staying away from the booze?"

"Best as I can," I told him.

"That's all we ask." Billy smiled. "That's all we ask."

"Billy, can I ask you something myself?" I said.

"Sure, I guess."

"How come you talk to me like you're wasting your breath?"

Billy rubbed the white bald spot on the top of his head and frowned. Some light made a halo right above that crown. "I generally am wasting it, I guess. There's not much hope for people to change the way they are."

"Sounds mighty uplifting."

"I'm not here to inspire, Lemay, I'm here to keep you outta jail. Go to a goddamn priest if you wanna be lied to. I've seen too many of your kind slip back inside to fool myself. If you wanna think you're a new man, hell, that's fine. But don't think you're looking any different in anyone else's mind."

I put out my cigarette and shook my head. "Any of your cons ever take a swing at you?"

Billy Blakes made a real smile this time and leaned in close. "Just once, Luce. Just once. Had him back inside so quick his goddamn head spun right off. Think he's still making license plates down in Marion, if my memory serves me right. Why, you feel like taking a swing at me?"

"If I thought I'd knock anything good loose."

Billy grinned and patted me on the back. "You got heart. I'll give you that. Dumb as a stump and doomed as hell, but you've got heart."

After that, I had the rest of the afternoon off, so I walked into town and had a sandwich at the Starlite in hopes of catching a sight of Charlene, but she was nowhere around, then I walked around town some more, and somehow I ended up over at this pink house. Right there, I decided I ought to just give in to all my poor lusty dreams. It wasn't a thing I could fight. It was something wicked and burning inside of me.

Dahlia and Favor Muller's house was a big white one with nice pink awnings and pink trim. It all looked like a nicely iced kind of confectionery. There was no car in the drive. No kids playing out in front. I burdened up my lust at the bottom of the stairs and walked up to the white front door. I pressed my finger to the doorbell and held my breath.

The door opened and Dahlia stood there grinning with her hand over her ample chest.

"Ask and you shall receive. Isn't that what the Good Book says? Just tell me this isn't a dream."

Dal was wearing this pretty little blue number, this blouse that stopped just short of her belly and a matching blue skirt, showing off her middle and her bare legs. I felt myself get nervous. I felt my hands get wet with moisture and my throat grow dry.

"Do you mind if I come in for a drink?" I muttered.

"I thought you'd never ask." She smiled with a little mischievous wink.

Dal opened the screen door before I really knew what I had just said. I stepped inside and looked around the front room. The first thing I noticed was the sofa. It was red, covered in clear vinyl or plastic, pretty large, set up against the wall. It had been on a couch like that where I had first kissed Dahlia, innocently or not so, I guess, just a kiss on the cheek when we were sixteen or so. It had been there that I had sealed my own fate. I was going to make the same hopeless mistake. Believe what this honey-toothed woman said. Believe all the things she laid so gently at my ear.

"Where's your husband?" I asked.

"At work. Where every husband should be. Collecting trash."

Dal sat down on the sofa, spreading her skirt over her bare, creamy legs. They were genuinely creamy. Everything about her was pretty creamy.

"Luce, I just need to get something off my chest."

I stared into her blue, blue eyes, wondering if it was not her blouse.

"I just need to tell you how sorry I am for putting you through all of that. I mean, the eloping and not being pregnant and all that."

I looked her in her white face. It had all been a lie. The worst one I had ever heard in my whole life. It was a thing that would not go away with a simple little apology. Poor Dahlia had told me she was with child. Pregnant by me, sure as hell. Dal told me if I didn't elope with her and skip town, then she'd go see the doctor in Colterville and get the problem fixed. Just like that. So I didn't have any real choice to make. I loved her and I loved the kid that wasn't even born, so I made off with the returns of the liquor store. But then there was the accident, and the trial, and me going to prison, and then after three months she finally told me it had all been a lie. Nothing more than a way of getting me to marry her and take her out of a town she had hated more than anything in the world. But it was too late. Three months of dreaming about having a child of my own. Watching the way Dahlia's belly never seemed to grow when she came to the prison to visit. Worrying myself sick that the poor little baby was ill somehow. Worrying that it would grow up wrong having its daddy sitting in prison.

"I'm sorry for all the pain I caused you." Dal sighed, pulling my hand against the side of her face. "I still love you so much. You have to know that. I love you more than I could love any other man."

Dal tilted her head to the side, closing her eyes. This meant she was ready to kiss. I felt my mouth go dry right away. Dal flashed open her blue eyes. Boy, she really had pretty eyes, they were deeper blue around the irises, cool and delicate, they weren't set too close together or too far apart. Dahlia patted the blank, empty sofa space beside her. I nodded and sat down. She placed her tiny white hand over my knee, leaning in close.

"I just knew you would come. I knew you could forgive me. I knew you would." She smiled, unbuttoning her skirt. I caught a quick glimpse of her smooth white flesh and the unholy tight blue panties beneath. I always liked the way that looked. I could paint a dozen goddamn masterpieces of "*Girl in Panties.*" I don't know why, maybe it was the mystery of it all, but seeing Dahlia in her underdrawers would always be enough to make me fold.

She had been waiting for this kiss a long time. I could feel it along her lips. She had dreamed of me coming back. She had been waiting for the kiss for almost three years. There was nothing but the tingling of her own lust against my skin. But there was no ardor there that belonged to me. No tenderness that made me want to open my eyes and stare into her unloving face.

Another lady held my heart in her hand. Charlene.

Then I could see all the lies that Dal had told me written somewhere upon her sweet skin. All the dishonesty and guilt seeping out of her flesh. And I knew something else, something clear as a bell. I had never forgiven her for all the things she had said.

"Dal," I whispered, "I can't."

"He won't be home for hours. He's out with the trash."

"It isn't Favor, it's me. It's me. It's someone else. I can't get her out of my head."

"What? But you can have me . . . right here . . . right now . . ."

"I know. That's the trouble with it all. My heart isn't here. I think somewhere deep inside I can tell I don't like you very much."

"Get out," Dal muttered. "Get out!"

I shot up from the couch, tripping over an end table, smacking my head on the couch. I stumbled out the front door as Dahlia began throwing things at me.

"You bastard!" she shouted. She pegged me with some stupid glass poodle, still baring only her underpants. The poodle cracked into a dozen pieces against the back of my head. I tripped down the front stairs and out to the street. I didn't notice until I was down the block that I was smiling. I felt blessed as hell all of a sudden. All of a sudden I knew how bad I wanted Charlene. All I could do was smile about it and whisper her name to myself again and again in surety.

knot in the flesh

A lonely drifting heart may find another of its kind to moor. That's what I was hoping for, at least. A delicate rope to keep me from floating adrift.

Viceroy cigs 1.50 pk
unfiltrd and penitent
as an only wish

At night, I stared out the dull glass windows up into Junior's electric sign. I began to close the gas station a few minutes early when these kids, these really young dirty-faced kids, came in. They had their blue baseball hats pulled down halfway covering their faces, their eyes looking at their feet. They weaseled up to the counter and stared me right in my eyes. This one kind of red-faced kid with freckles and red hair nodded at me. The other one with greasy black hair and real pink lips dropped the money on the counter.

"Pack of Viceroy Golds," the kid with freckles whispered, staring down from the blackness beneath his baseball hat.

I smiled, shaking my head. "You got ID?" I asked.

"Nope," the kid mumbled, not moving away from the

counter. I looked down into that red-faced kid, right into his little eyeballs, and shook my head.

"Sorry, kid. I already told you. Try some other place."

"Man, don't be a dick. Just give us the smokes."

"Get the hell outta here before I come around the counter and brain you both."

They shook their heads, hitting each other in the arm.

"Asshole!" the red-faced kid shouted. He slammed the glass door closed, still swearing and shaking his head. I smiled and came out from behind the counter and locked the doors, then closed down the station, cleaning and restocking, switching off the lights and pumps. I turned the signs off and folded my blue Gas-N-Go hat and slipped it in my rear jeans pocket. Then I stepped outside into the warm blue night. The night was sweet and clean-smelling like a prom bouquet. I just stood there for a second and smiled, staring up at the sky.

"There he is!!" someone shouted from the blackness.

"Asshole!!!" someone else yelled.

A big wad of dirt flew through the black night, crossing down, and hit the glass door behind me. I had just cleaned the windows that day. I turned back around, squinting into the dark.

"Get 'im!!!" someone shouted.

"Asshole!!!"

There was another volley of dirt. Three or four clumps smacked the glass windows and doors behind me. One lucky clump caught me right in the forehead, sent from the cover of darkness. I squinted my eyes and peeked behind the dull fluorescent streetlights and saw about a half-dozen little bastards lined up behind the first line of gas pumps, armed with a big gray plastic bucket full of dirt.

"Asshole!!!" the kids shouted. It was the goddamn cigarette kids. I could see that lousy little red face as another dried clump of dirt caught me in the ear. They all laughed and kept throwing, smacking the glass behind me, haw-hawing through their miserable little teeth and dirty mouths. Then the front of the glass Coca-Cola machine suddenly shattered with shards and bits of rocks and dirt. That was it. I saw that happen and ran right for one of them. He gave a little cry as he froze where he stood, shrinking up in on himself as I grabbed him around his tiny arm. The other kids shouted and took off, leaving this one kid all by himself. It was the one with red hair and splotchy red freckles. His face was so tight and full of fear that he looked ready to cry.

"Broke the goddamn Coke machine!" I shouted. "Little punk!!"

"Don't brain me," he muttered, his eyes watering with tears. "Sweet Jesus, I'll come back tomorrow and clean it all up. I swear. It was just a joke. I'll come back and clean it up and pay fer it to be fixed."

I let go of his arm and turned him loose. He ran off into the dark. I stood there for a minute, looking at the mess. There was dirt all over the front windows. Bits of plastic and glass strewn along the front of the Coke machine. I gave a little mumble to myself. It was a mess. There was no way in hell that kid was coming back. It had felt like the right thing to do, turning that kid loose. But there was no way he was coming back. I shook my head and frowned and began picking up the broken glass. I went back inside and got myself a broom and some towels and started whistling to myself to keep from getting mad as hell. It took me two hours to clean it up. By then it was nearly midnight. I began to walk down the road, still whistling to myself. A huge white moon hung low and heavy in the sky. The rest of the night sky was black and thin, like a sheet, it slipped around the moon like a nice black frame. It was very beautiful is all I can rightly say.

Don't ask me how or why, but I ended up at the Starlite Diner again. I stood outside the joint and stared in through the glossy white glass windows. It was hot and warm. I looked in through a side window, shading the light from my eyes with my hands, and stared inside.

Charlene saw me and looked up from the shiny white counter, just lifting her head a little. She smiled a low sad smile, like she was forgiving something, then looked back down at her white, white hands. Her brown hair was so curly. It twisted and ran all over her shoulders. She leaned closer against the counter as I walked around the front of the diner and inside. My chest felt weak and heavy all at once. I marched right up to the counter and took a red vinyl seat at the bar without even knowing what I wanted to say.

"Hi," she kind of whispered. Her hair smelled so good and heavy and sweet. She pushed some of it behind her ear and leaned closer over the counter.

"How do." I smiled, staring down at my hands.

"Are you going to order anything tonight?" she asked curtly. Her eyes were cold and stinging and brown.

"No," I mumbled, giving her an awful look back, still kind of smiling a little.

"You can't just come and sit here. You'll get me in trouble."

"Fine," I grinned, swiveling on the red vinyl stool. "What do I care?"

"You're really some sorta jerk, aren't you? Don't you have anything better to do than bother me?"

I shrugged my shoulders. "No, not really." I looked down at my hands as I ran my fingers in big wide circles across the counter. I twisted a paper napkin between them. I poured a tiny mound of salt and began sifting it back and forth nervously.

"Jerk," she murmured with a small smile, rolling her eyes. "What do want from me?" she finally asked.

I wanted to touch the back of her neck. "Nothing," I murmured. I looked around the diner. The same trucker with the same red beard was in the same seat. Maybe he hadn't ever left.

"Why do you come here then?" She said it mean, because it was supposed to be mean. "Can't you find some other girl to bother?"

"Don't you have something to do here?" I asked, looking around again. "That guy looks like he can use another slice of pie."

"Don't *you* have something to do?" Charlene asked.

"Forget it!" I shouted, knocking the tiny mound of salt across the counter. "You're just a dumb kid." I hopped off the stool and strode outside, slamming the glass door open hard. It shook in the frame, but didn't break or anything.

I looked up at the lousy low yellow moon and spun around as the door opened behind me and her clean white legs shone in the dark.

"Maybe . . ." she whispered, her heels clicked against the pavement. "Maybe we can go out sometime." Charlene smiled. She was holding my hand. "But I'm telling you right now, this isn't a date or anything. I have to work every night until two." She sighed.

"That's fine." I smiled. "I can meet you tonight after work if you'd like."

"OK. But this isn't a date."

"No." I nodded. "Nothing like that."

She kind of looked at me, biting her lip, then over my shoulder at the moon, then back at me. My heart was pounding against the inside of my dirty gas station shirt. All I could see was her pink, pink lips, lit up by the moon. I was holding her hand again, don't ask me how, but we were just standing there, holding hands really weakly, just by the fingertips like it was the only thing keeping us there on earth.

"Don't you want to kiss me?" she asked.

"What?" I mumbled, like I hadn't been thinking about it all along.

"Don't you want to kiss me? I mean, I think you woulda walked away if you didn't wanna kiss me now."

We kissed. The kiss tasted like summer and spring. It was by far a beautiful kiss because we didn't stop kissing for a long time. She reached her hand against the back of my sweaty neck, the smell of her hair swimming all around my head, her lips soft against mine, my eyes closed because that's the way I like to kiss, our noses kind of rubbing against one another. I touched her pink-blue dress, feeling her tongue in my mouth, I touched her side as she bit my bottom lip and pulled away, disappearing back into the diner before I could say another sweet word.

I ran home to the hotel smiling and jumping like a loon, because I could still smell her hair and her mouth had felt good and there was nothing to make a fool feel better than something beautiful like lust. I went home and showered and changed and ate what Old Lady St. Francis had left on the stove for me, chipped beef and some ungodly vegetables that stunk of earthly decay. Then I ran back down the streets toward the dim white lights of the Starlite Diner, trying to keep myself from sweating, trying to keep myself from smiling like some sort of madman. I peeked in the diner through a side window and smiled. Charlene was bent over a cooler of some kind, pulling out a cold cherry pie. Her skirt kind of crept up her legs to her rear, and I saw where her nude nylons ended and her real skin began. Nice all right. There was a thin, peach-colored line of flesh that moved beneath her dress, just above her nylons. I smiled, shaking my head, and then rubbed my eyes. I waited outside by some parked cars. I laid my head down on the curb between a big gray Ford and a little red Chevy and stared up at the cool blue night sky until Charlene finally came out in her little pink-blue dress. I had been looking right up at the Big Dipper or Little Dipper or maybe not even a dipper at all, and when I looked up and saw her standing over me smiling, her face was all lit with the stars.

"Cute." She grinned, pulling me to my feet. "Let's go."

This was the first time I noticed it, but she was taller than me. I felt myself sink. This girl was goddamn taller than me. She must have been thinking the same thing, because she kind of smiled and squinted her eyes and looked at me, then backed away.

"I didn't think you were short." She smiled.

"What?"

"I didn't know hoods were so short."

"That's nice. Maybe you're just a tall kinda goonie," I murmured like my feelings were hurt. They weren't hurt, but that's something you have to do when you're really thinking about kissing a tall pretty girl.

"Maybe you're just a hog boy." She smiled, crossing her arms in front of her chest. "A hoodlum with a hog's face."

"Listen, maybe this was a mistake . . ." I mumbled. My mouth began to form another word, but she kissed me before I could say it.

"Let's go." Charlene smiled. She dug into the wide white pocket of her dress and pulled out her car keys, then dangled them from her long white finger.

"Where we going?"

"You'll see," she giggled. This was nice. This was all I wanted. Something nice like this. She unlocked the door to a big blue Ford and hopped in the driver's seat, then leaned over and pulled up the tiny silver lock, and started the car.

"My mom said she came in and got gas from you and you didn't say hello." Charlene smiled, pulling the car away. I thought about Mrs. Dulaire. She had come in to get gas, but I had pretended not to remember her in any way.

This Mrs. Dulaire was definitely a crazy. She always carried this poodle under her arm wherever she went. It was this little gray yipping thing that would snarl and hiss and bark from the folds of Mrs. Dulaire's weighty arms, like a kind of animate little detached head.

"Did your mother say something to me?" I asked.

"No." She smiled. I liked the way Charlene drove. Her eyes were real wide. Her hands were tight at ten and two on the steering wheel, like she had just learned how to drive. Real attentive.

"How come she didn't say hello to me then?" I asked, with a big dumb smile. "What type of woman wouldn't say hello to the poor gas attendant on duty?"

"She thinks you're a hood, too." Charlene flashed me her smile. "That's what they call you. A hood."

"Do you think I give a shit what your crazy mother thinks of me?" I blurted out. That was the problem with me. Something might sure sound funny in my head, but then after I said it, I realized it really sounded bad. Charlene kind of shrunk up, shaking her head a little, her eyes got a little dull then shiny, then she acted like I wasn't even there.

"Do you think that's funny or something?" she shot out suddenly. "Because it isn't. I remember your family. Your family isn't great or anything."

I kind of smiled because I was the first one to admit that, but it sounded like a kid thing to say. "I'm sorry," I whispered, staring out the side window.

I had no idea where we were going. We were going somewhere, though, I could tell, Charlene was definitely driving somewhere. Then I thought maybe the whole thing was a bad idea, about her mother the crazy poodle lady and all. If anything did happen between us, I'd have to say hello to her mother every time she came in, not just say hello, but be a real polite bastard, like it didn't hurt me to sit there and talk to her and know she knows I'm making her daughter. The whole thing suddenly looked like a bad idea.

"I heard you ran into Earl." Charlene frowned. Her eyes flashed all silver and brown.

"How's that?"

"He came in and told me. Said he was the one that busted up your face. I'm awful sorry about that. I thought he'd be a little more mature about the whole thing. You can see why I decided to break it off." Charlene nodded to herself, biting her bottom lip. "Well, I'm sorry about it anyway."

"Not as sorry as me." I smiled. Charlene smiled back. I felt like we had been dating all our lives.

"Where we headed anyway?" I asked.

"Here," she whispered, pulling the car over to the curb. She switched off the lights and lifted her finger to her mouth. "Be quiet, though," she sighed. I shrugged my shoulders and opened the car door. There was the Boneyard River, stretched out all dark and blue and mumbling quietly to itself. There were some weeping willows and tall green grass wavering like words in the river's breath.

"What are we doing here?" I asked.

"Shh." She smiled and grabbed my hand. There was something I liked about that, her grabbing my hand all the time. Charlene led me down the side of the bank to where the cold dark water rose against the muddy earth. There were cattails and sticker-bushes and tiger lilies growing there, moving gently in time to the movement the river made as it muttered along.

"Take off your clothes," she whispered.

I froze where I was. Charlene unzipped her blue-pink dress. I didn't know what to think. I began to unbuckle my pants. She slipped off her shoes and dropped the dress at her feet. Her bare white skin shone and glimmered, moving under a dull white bra and panties that cut across the top of her legs. She slipped into the dark river, shivering, then covered her chest, bobbing up and down, giggling to herself.

I had no idea what the hell to think. I was afraid my goddamn erection was about to burst from my drawers, but I tore off my pants anyway, dropped them down around my ankles, but then remembered I had forgotten to take off my shoes. I jerked my pants back up and tore them off. I stepped out of my pants and yanked my shirt off and jumped into the river, making a big splash.

"Shh!!" She smiled, splashing some water at me. The water was freezing, but it smelled nice, nice and clean and pungent like dirt. There was no sound. Nothing. There were tiny white bugs that fluttered all over the place, tiny white and yellow gnats and bugs that flew in wide white circles. I moved in front of Charlene. Her dark brown hair hung all wet over her smooth white shoulders, as all the white bugs circled like thin halos over her head. I stared into her eyes and couldn't think a single thing except how perfect they were. I felt like I might just suddenly drift straight downstream. I felt light and weak and hollow as a twig. I moved right up to her and started kissing her and held her close right in the water, and she kissed me back, holding me around the neck. Her lips were broad and flat and broad and soft and broad. Her mouth never stopped moving. I felt my teeth chattering, but I didn't care. She kissed me hard on the mouth once more, then pulled herself out of the water and walked up the bank quietly. I liked the way she moved. Real slow and careful, like she always knew I was looking at her.

"This way." She wrung her curly brown hair out over the water, squeezed it and a thousand tiny drops of water flashed back down. She picked up her dress and purse and shoes, then turned and walked along the dark green bank to an old gray boathouse that rose like an assembly of fallen trees a few yards away. She motioned to me. I pulled myself out of the water. My heart was pounding like a madman. I stumbled over a soft gray log. Charlene shook her head and opened the sliding door. She walked inside and then sat down in an old gray rowboat, rocking it a little as she moved. There were thousands of shiny silver cobwebs stretching out overhead, trembling with tiny beads of water in their threads. There was a wave of humidity that covered everything, pulling us close. I shut the sliding door.

Charlene threw her arms around my head, pulling me on top, kissing me some more. Her hair was warm against my face. The old rowboat rocked as I ran my hand along her side, down her back. I touched her bare legs and slipped my hand along the back of thighs. Her lips moved all over my face and neck, her hand slipped over my shoulder, up my chest, then down. She slipped her fingers under my drawers, then slowly, slowly, she slid my boxers down a little. I wasn't even breathing.

My hand climbed up to her behind, then her breast. My other hand moved down and over her wet white panties, down, then over and up, between her thighs.

"OK, wait," she murmured.

I felt my chest become hard.

She sat up and slipped open her black purse and pulled out a condom wrapped in silver foil, and placed it in my hand.

My god.

We did it, right there, in that old boathouse, as if we had done it all the time together before. We laid on top of each other, together in this old rowboat, moving slowly, then fast, then not at all. This girl was as sweaty as me, and I liked that. Her face and forehead, her hands, her mouth was hot against mine and a little stale. I could make out a tiny red mark along her hairline and a tiny blemish beside her lip, but none of that . . . mattered to me. We laid there staring at each other, not saying a word, lit up by the low moonlight through the slots in the roof, holding each other tight against the old soft wood. The stars moved gently overhead, slipping past quietly, shining down in her eyes. It was the closest I had felt to anything in a long time. I felt like I wasn't drifting downstream.

clout

Charlene made me feel full of fire and life. But most other things made me feel like a man who was grave as hell. Like Monte Slates. He walked into the Gas-N-Go all beaten up one Saturday afternoon. The boy who bought the rubbers to use as water balloons to drop off the overpass on La Harpie Road. His eye was all swelled up and black-and-blue. He nodded at me as I handed him the bathroom key and stared hard at his sore little face.

"What happened there, kid, drop a balloon on the sheriff's squad car?"

"Nope. My old man gave it to me."

"Your old man? What for?" I asked.

"Stealing quarters from his coffee can."

"Well, how many did you take?"

"Eight or nine, I guess." He frowned.

"Eight or nine?" Jesus. The thought of this kid's old man beating on him like that made me sick.

"Two bucks ain't worth no black eye," Junior whispered. He was keeping me company during my shift. "Daddy that beats on his kid like that ain't right."

"Pal, where is it you live?" I asked. I was about to do something. Maybe something that wasn't so much for the kid, but for me.

"My daddy don't have any feet."

"How's that?" Junior frowned.

"My daddy don't have any feet. He don't like to talk to anybody because of his feet."

Monte's old man had lost both his feet to gangrene during the Vietnam War. They got amputated right off and buried in a shallow grave like old lovers. Now he had plastic feet: hard and pink and without any real shape. He had to have been in the same bad mood since they cut his poor toes and heels off.

"Get off my porch!" I heard the old man shout through the dull white front door as soon as my feet touched the steps.

I had walked a few blocks over to Monte's house. He had told me where he lived as soon as I promised not to start any trouble. The house was a big and gray, with a wire fence and brown-black lawn. The gate had been left open. There was a carburetor and some other auto parts lying on a blue tarp on the front porch. I went up the walk to the front door and held my breath. I had no idea what I was going to say. I knocked just once. My shoulders tightened. A cool, dull light beamed from under the front door. I knocked again, then I stepped back from the door. It was completely silent. I knocked on the door once more and this time I heard the cheap locks undoing themselves and the cold clatter of it all. Monte's old man swung the door open as far as the tiny gold security chain would give.

His face was ugly. Not interesting ugly, not out of the ordinary, I mean. His face was plain and rotten from the inside. An ugliness that grew from the heart and weak blood. He jammed his face between the door. His black hair was greasy and graying.

"Where's the goddamn fire?" Monte's old man asked. "And who the hell are you?"

"Name's Luce Lemay. I came to talk about your boy."

"Christ Jesus, what's that kid done now?" He squinted his

eyes, then nodded, and closed the door, unlocking the security chain. He opened the door again and I stepped inside. I dug my fists into my pants pockets, trying not to stare at his plastic feet. I looked around. The inside of the house was warm and awful-smelling. I could see an open bottle of sour mash from across the room and a rotten old sandwich, decomposing on a coffee table with only three working legs. I looked at Mr. Slates's face again. He looked like hell. He patted me on the shoulder and turned, without saying a word, and wobbled toward the bathroom with his canes, shifting his weight from side to side. He made it inside and closed the door behind.

The place was completely dark, except for the blue flicker of the TV. I could hear the buzz and flick as it switched from clear-ness to static. Monte's old man kept coughing in the john, tearing up the back of his throat. He must have been doubled over the toi-let, sick with liquor, I guess. He flushed and stepped out, wiping his slick mouth with the back of his hand. I nodded as he wobbled over and took a seat on the dirty gray flannel couch. He swore at the bugs and swatted at the rotten sandwich with his big hand.

"Damn bugs," he muttered, then gripped the open, half-emptied bottle of sour mash and took a long swig.

"I know you, don't I? Where do I know you from?" he mut-tered to the darkness around my head.

"I dunno. I work at the gas station down the street."

Mr. Slates scratched his whiskered face, then nodded to him-self. He snapped his fingers together hard, then pointed right at me.

"I know you. I knowed your daddy. You're the boy that ran that baby down."

"How's that?" I mumbled.

"You're the boy that ran that baby down a few years back. Lemay? Tough break that was, pal. Running that baby down like that."

"It was an accident. It was all a mistake."

"That's what I thought. Looks like the jury saw it different." Mr. Slates rolled himself a smoke, packing the tobacco tight into the paper sleeve. He lit the cigarette and let the smoke roll around his head. "So what the hell are you doing in my house?" Monte's old man grunted, staring at the TV.

I felt my tongue grow hard, my fingers clench tight into fists. "I came to talk about your son."

"My son? My son? What's that boy gone off and done now?"

"Nothing. Nothing at all. It's about what's been done to him."

"What are you talking about?"

"Came into the gas station with a sore eye and busted lip. Said his daddy was the one that gave it to him."

"That so?" Monte's old man took a short swig of sour mash and swished it from cheek to cheek. "What's this got to do with you, pal?"

"Nothing, I guess. Just don't think you beating on a young boy like that is right."

"That so? I guess running down babies makes you an expert, huh?"

I shook my head quick, trying to knock something loose.

"I wanted to come talk to you first, before I got hold of the police."

"You call the police!" he yelled. "They'll have a real goddamn laugh. You coming here and telling me how to raise my kid."

"Just keep your damn hands off the boy," I muttered, tightening my fingers into fists.

"I'll treat my boy as I see fit." His eyes were dark and full of ignorant pride.

"You won't bruise that boy again, you hear? You won't hit that boy again or I swear I'll come back."

"Big words from a goddamned lousy convict."

Then something snapped.

I went over and grabbed that fucker by his throat and shoved him down hard against the ground, knocking over his booze. I could hear his plastic pink feet clicking together in fear.

"Listen to me, fucker. Keep your damn hands off of that boy, you understand? You let that boy grow up by himself fair."

I let go of his throat and stepped out on the porch and tried to light a cigarette as quick as I could. My hands were trembling too hard. The goddamn matches kept flashing out. Finally, I lit it and choked the smoke down my throat. I wanted to go back in and crack that bastard hard in his chin. But it wouldn't have done any good. This Mr. Slates was a man I had seen my whole life. He was lost as any man could ever be, and nothing, no lousy fistfight, would change that.

"Didn't hit my dad, didja?" Monte asked. He was sitting on the front porch steps, with his head hung low in his lap.

"No." I frowned, taking a long drag on my smoke. "We just sat down and had ourselves a talk."

"A talk, huh? That was all?"

"Sure it was. It's all clear now. He said he's gonna keep from hitting you from now on."

Monte just sucked in a low breath and shook his head and stared up at his dilapidated old porch. The blue light from the TV flickered in his tiny blue eyes.

"Didn't change anything, did it?" he asked.

The cigarette smoke turned cold in my mouth. There was nothing different I could have done myself. I wanted to go in there and break his goddamn teeth. I wanted to call the goddamn police. But I had lost all of my words.

I was like a ghost, cursed to do nothing but stand alone and watch and try to utter a word in help, but forlorn, forlorn by a silence I could not control.

"Doesn't seem like your dad has his head on that straight," I said. "I don't know what to tell you, pal. Don't know what to say. If he lays a hand on you like that again, you let me know and I'll talk to him again."

"Thanks," Monte mumbled, starting up the porch.

I flicked out the cigarette and walked away, trying to make it right in my head by saying it a different way.

the red ventricle along the wall

The Virgin's breath revealed a hole in a dark-lit soul. A hole that began to show some light onto the unknown face of a friend.

The Virgin took a breath, moving along the wall of my room.

I stared at that beautiful painting all morning. Then I got a notion. Something struck me funny. I got up from the black frame bed and lifted the Virgin right off the wall. Some dust settled to my feet. Some strange light seemed to break right through.

There was a hole dug right in that wall straight from Junior's room, reaching through. A hole filled with mysterious things he had placed there to keep hidden. I set the painting on the floor and stared inside, squinting my eyes. These were all things kept close to Junior's heart. Things I had only heard about but never seen.

The baby bird's two black eyes. I saw them right away. They were all dried up and hard and kept between two pieces of green glass. They flickered there dull and lifeless but still full of some kind of sight.

There was an old Bowie knife. A ball of white string. A piece of chalk and an old red leather dictionary, torn at the binding. I opened up the dictionary and saw a marking right under the front cover. It had been stolen from Colterville Elementary School. I set it back in place as something else caught my eye.

There was an old photograph placed in that dark cubbyhole. It was one of the strangest pictures I had ever seen. It was black-and-white and mostly out of focus, grayed along the edges and wrinkled in certain spaces around the center. It was a photo of a girl with two round cheeks and closed eyes surrounded by flowers on all sides, lying on her back in the dirt. This girl was smiling the biggest smile I had ever seen. Her little stubby teeth were all unwrapped under her chubby round lips and gray gums. She had on a nice white dress and colored ribbons strung up in her dark curly hair. There was some writing along the back of the picture that gave away the girl's name. *EUNICE*, it read in firm capital letters. *EUNICE*. This girl *EUNICE* was like a little princess of the garden. She couldn't have been more than thirteen. Her cheeks were still chubby with baby fat. I held that photo in my hand a long time. I wondered if it was an old girlfriend of Junior's. His first love maybe.

I put all the things back in the hole in the wall right before I noticed there was a huge wad of cash all rolled up, jammed into another opening. There had to have been a few hundred dollars there, just hidden away, tied up tight with white string and nestled in a crack. I gave a little smile thinking of Junior keeping all those things like that, kind of like a little kid, hiding all his most precious things in a hole behind a painting. I put the Virgin back into place, got dressed for work, and headed on out.

There was a new message on that shiny silver sign out front of the gas station.

Auto repair done cheap
in-expensive as a trip
down a lusterd stream

I squinted a little as I read it, then stepped inside. Junior was behind the counter, staring at the wall. His round face looked tired and worn.

"How do, pal?" I smiled, stepping around the counter.

"Not so good, Luce, not so good."

"Looks like you haven't slept in a week."

"Not that long. Just the last few days is all."

"What do you think it is?" I asked.

"I dunno. Something running loose in my head. I can fall asleep all right, but then I have these dreams and I end up waking up and just lying there the rest of the night. I dunno. I can't sleep in those rooms all alone. I keep hearing things."

"Hearing things? The guy above me has a lady over almost every night." I smiled.

"No, I keep hearing something in the room with me. Whispering . . . whispering something to me from the closet all night."

I looked up into Junior's wide white face.

"You know there's nothing in that room with you. It's all your imagination, pal."

"It's hard to think of that when you're sure something's breathing down your neck." Junior stepped out from around the counter.

"Where you headed?" I asked.

"Take a walk, I guess. Maybe down to the river. Set my mind at some ease."

"Good luck, pal. I'll bring home some whiskey tonight to help you sleep."

"Thanks."

His large feet led him right to the river's edge. It was warm and sticky along his skin. Some insects muttered little songs to themselves. The water was green and heavy and dark. He could see his own reflection, cast dismal and black, moving right under the surface. He leaned over and lowered his hand, making the two Juniors meet.

Then he was gone.

He set the saw against her left shinbone first.

He closed his eyes and took in a deep breath. Then he began to move. A little at first, then in a steady, unyielding stroke, running the saw's blade against the skin, back and forth, back and forth, until the tendons and muscles gave and the tiny gray foot dropped right off. It fell into the dirt with a quiet little stirring sound. He opened his eyes quick, then placed the sawblade against her right shin and began to cut.

He would fix it all right.

He would make everything all right.

He cut off her other foot and dropped it in the black plastic bag, then tied it tight.

Blood dripped down along his big white hands.

He placed the sawblade against her middle, closed his eyes, and set his body into motion against her fragile weight. The blade made it through the flesh in quick, clean strokes, severing the tissue and bone, moving through her innards and flesh with a gluttonous wet sound, on down, on down, splitting her spine. Then she was undone. Right in two. Two nearly equal halves, two souls of her own. He slipped her belly-mess into the bag and then began to undo her lower half, splitting apart her thin gray hips. Then her legs, and hands, and her head from her neck. Then it had all been done. Then she had been unmade like an old sweater or broken toy and he had separated all the pieces into different bags, leaving her head and torso nearly intact. He lit the match and poured the gasoline over the bags evenly. They began to smolder and burn, shrinking in on themselves, twisting and turning into fleshy black knots that flickered with flames. He placed the burning bags on the tiny wood raft, then returned to the shed and stared at her middle and face. There were flies all over her skin, buzzing and hissing about, stealing tiny beads of sweat from her closed eyes.

He took the hammer and held it tight in his hands. He held it tight and square and stared hard at her shiny white teeth, then closed his eyes and took a solid, momentous swing, then again, then once more, making sure there would be no way to trace, no way to identify the parts of her body once they began to wash up from the river somewhere downstream. He placed her head and torso on the tiny little wood raft, then lit the match and poured out the rest of the gasoline and gave it all a good push and watched it slip slowly down the stream, drifting away, disappearing down, down, down into the cold green murk once it was taken up by the current. He dug up the bloody dirt with his fingers and wiped the place clean with an old gas-can rag, then buried it all somewhere beneath the woodshed and closed the door.

He held the hammer tight in his hands. He nailed the woodshed shut and walked with the tool alone through the dark.

It was all done.

It was all done.

He was in his own room now. Now he was standing before his closet door and had Old Lady St. Francis's hammer and seven nails in his hands and pounded the spikes through the closet door into the frame, nailing it shut tight and good. Then the next nail, straight through the door into the frame, cracking the wood a little as he slammed the hammer harder and harder against the head of the nail. Then the next, then the next, and so on, until the dull black closet door had been nailed shut and tight. Then poor ol' Junior fell on the floor and placed the end of one of the nails against his forearm and dug a new hole, a new word, drawing his blood through the letters and his skin.

STAY.

He was crying hard now, gripping his arm tight, as he bled all over the wood floor and his clothes and wrapped an old shirt around his arm and held it there until he had himself burrowed between the tiny wire bed and the space along the wall.

At eleven o'clock there was no sound coming from his room. I knocked on the door once, then gave the knob a turn and stepped inside. There was poor ol' Junior curled up in a ball between the bed and the wall.

"Christ, Junior, are you all right?" I asked, switching on the lightbulb.

"Fine," he whispered. "Go away. I'm fine."

"Like hell you are," I muttered. "What the hell is all this? Blood? Blood? Where's all this blood from?"

There was a quiet little smattering of blood all over Junior's clothes and dried up along the dull wood floor.

"Christ Jesus, Junior, are you OK?" I stood over him, shaking my head. Then I saw the letters along his fleshy white arm. I saw the word the letters spelled out.

STAY.

"What the hell is that?" I asked. "Christ, Junior, get up off the floor and let me take a look at that cut."

"No," he mumbled. "It's mine."

Then I knew what this poor fool was talking about right away.

STAY.

Poor old Junior wanted to keep that pain and anguish all to himself. He wanted it to live and breathe and speak inside of him.

I looked down at his face. It was all round and caked in blood and sweat.

"Here," I whispered, placing the bottle of whiskey on his bed. "Have a drink with me. We'll stay up and talk this all out."

"No," Junior replied softly. "It's too late. It's already too late."

"Too late?" I tried to smile. "What are you talking about, too late?"

"Don't you see, Luce, we've already made our mistakes. The worst mistakes anyone can make. Nothing can make us whole again."

Big Junior Breen was trembling. He began to cry again, burying his face into the side of the bed.

"Junior . . ." I started to whisper. But there was nothing else I could say. I reached out my hand and patted him on his back, then stepped away and into my room.

I lay down on the bed. I tried to close my eyes. I thought about the letters on Junior's arm all night. I could feel the wounds moving there within my own heart.

The draft along the wall kept shaking the Virgin Mary's frame and I could hear Junior crying and mumbling to himself until sometime in the morning when I finally fell asleep.

In that early-morning light, Junior pulled himself up off the floor. He lifted the Virgin Mary painting off the wall and took all the things he had hidden there. He strode out of his room and down the hall and outside and down to the banks of the Boneyard River.

Junior walked right to the edge of the river, clopping through the high brown grass. His boots were full of mud now. He was sweating a little as the sun began to peek out over the trees and reflect down on the shiny blue-green river as it muddled on past. Junior squatted in place, staring as the water rushed up to the ends of his boots. Then he placed each object—the twine, the baby bird's eyeballs (he threw the dictionary and the knife)—one by one and watched them drift and disappear down the river, sinking and growing darker as they vanished beneath the wake. Then he held the photograph of *EUNICE* in his big hands, smearing it with all the sweat and grease from his fingertips. He took a deep breath and placed it along the water's rippling edge, then pulled his hand away. The photograph took off, sailing downstream, twisting and turning as it moved along beside the bank. Junior gave a little whimper, then shook his head and chased after it, whimpering and murmuring as it sailed downstream, disappearing farther and farther down the bank. The picture could not go. He needed her face.

"Mmph," Junior whispered, getting his shoes all muddy and wet. He nearly tripped over a wet log and some high bank grass that itched beside his waist, fighting to keep the photograph in sight. He scrambled down the river's bank and lunged, slipping into the river up to his thick knees, catching the tiny gray image in his big white hand. He looked at it quickly, then stuck it in his shirt pocket and pulled himself out of the river, huffing and heaving as the cold water soaked through his clothes.

"Looks like you fell in all right, mister," a little voice bloomed. Junior looked up and gave a little smile to a tiny girl in a pink dress a few feet away who was sailing a little boat on the end of a string.

"Looks that way." Junior frowned, staring at his wet clothes. His shoes squeaked with water as he stepped down the bank.

"Is it cold?" the little girl asked.

"Sure is." Junior frowned again. "You best stay out of it."

"I aim to." The girl smiled. "But my boat sure likes it a lot."

"Looks like it does, all right."

"My name's Mary Margo Underlein. I live down the road."

"Is that so? My name's Junior. Junior Breen."

"That's a silly name." Mary Margo smiled.

"It sure is. I pray for a new one every night but it just hasn't come yet."

"My dad says I got to pray every night before bed to get the things I want. He says I gotta hold my hands together tight and pray for all the things I need, and if it's a good thing, it's bound to come true."

"Your daddy sounds like a smart man."

"He is. He built me this boat and painted it yellow. That takes smarts to do."

"I'll say." Junior smiled. Then he looked up and froze where he stood. There was the sheriff sitting in his squad car, shaking his head to himself real slow, shaking his head and mumbling something. He had been watching Junior all along. Junior looked away, feeling the sweat bead along the back of his neck. He stared out across the water to the sailboat, feeling the heat of the sheriff's gaze upon his bones.

"Look at it go," Mary Margo giggled.

The little yellow boat sailed along, drifting downstream, creating a tiny wake as it passed. Junior patted the girl on the head with a frown.

"I have to go now."

"Why?" Mary Margo asked.

"Just do, sweetheart."

"Can't you stay for a little while longer? I'll let you sail the boat if you want."

"Sorry, kiddo. I've got to go now."

"You have to go to work or something?"

"That's exactly where I have to go."

"Don't forget to say your prayers tonight." She smiled.

"How's that?" Junior asked.

"Before you go to bed tonight. Don't forget to say 'em so you get yourself a new name."

"I won't." He patted her soft straw hair again and walked away, staring up into the empty space where the sheriff's squad car had been. He headed down the road hoping he left no wake where his feet moved, holding the photograph in his hand as he walked toward work, not leaving a trace of his own weight upon the ground.

the fair queen of all corn

How far Charlene and I would tread from making it secretly in the backseat of her car to some sort of arranged relationship where we could manage to speak in a public way was as unsure as a poor nervous knock on her parent's thick wood door. But I took that chance anyway. I marched right up their nice front walk and up their porch and knuckled a nervous little report on their door without receiving any invitation at all.

"Is Charlene home?" I asked as soon as Mrs. Dulaire had the front door opened. Her bottom lip trembled a little as she gazed at my face. Mrs. Dulaire had raised six daughters and girded up the Used Car King of the Greater Southern Illinois Area. It had left little wrinkles around her pretty brown eyes and thin red lips. Those little lines of care made her seem sensitive and sweet as hell. But now her bottom lip would not stay in place.

"Charlene?" she murmured, still stunned. "'Course she is, Luce . . . just . . . one . . . moment . . . please . . ."

Mrs. Dulaire stared at me, then shook her head and backed away from the door. "Charlene!" she screamed, trying to swallow all the strange discomfort in her voice. "Charlene!!!"

Mrs. Dulaire smiled and nodded again, looking at my face. "She'll be right down," she whispered, cocking her head. She leaned against the thick white wood door, still peering at my face. "How have you been, Luce?" she asked. Mrs. Dulaire had always been nice to me. Mostly, she was just kind of crazy. She never made me feel bad for being me, a farm boy without much chance in the world to do a lot other than ruin the daughters of nice folk like her. I suddenly felt bad for not saying hello to her the time she came in for gas.

But Mr. Dulaire was another story. He was a man who held me in the highest of contempt. "Who's at the door, Virginia?" I heard him call from the smoking chair in the other room. "Is that Earl come to make up?"

I shook my head, trying to swallow all the spit down from my mouth.

"It's Luce," Mrs. Dulaire mumbled.

"How's that?"

"It's Luce," she replied. "Luce Lemay. Here to see Charlene."

"What's that?" he grumbled. I could hear the old man give a little grunt and pull himself out of his soft red chair and stroll on over to the front door. There he was all right. Mr. Milford Dulaire, the Used Car King, stared me hard in my face and nodded to himself. He wore a dull beige-and-brown sports jacket.

"Didn't know you were back in town, Luce," he said. "Thought you were still up in the tank."

"I got out a little while ago," I replied.

"That so? Is all that worked out now?"

"Reckon so." I frowned and looked down at the faded black-and-red tattoos along my arms. They looked old.

"Good, good, glad to see you out," he lied. His beige tie was making me ill. "So you find yourself a job yet?"

"I work nights over at the Gas-N-Go." I smiled.

"That's something." He nodded. "So." He tried to smile. "What is it you mean to see Charlene about?"

I stalled a little, taking a breath. "Just seeing if she planned on attending the fair tonight."

"That so? Well, I don't rightly know if she does or not."

"Mean to ask her myself." I grinned.

"Huh." He frowned. "That you do, huh?"

He rubbed the bald spot on the top of his head and then leaned in close to me. "All right, Luce. What is it you want with Charlene?"

I stared him hard in the face.

"Why you gonna go and foul up the head of another one of my poor daughters on me?" Mr. Dulaire asked.

I just shook my head and stared at my feet.

"Milford!" Mrs. Dulaire whispered. "Hush! You have to excuse Mr. Dulaire, Luce. He hasn't been the same since they took his hunting license away."

"That ain't it, Virginia." Mr. Dulaire frowned. "We just got a loyalty to Earl is all. He's almost our son-in-law and we couldn't just put him out like that."

Mrs. Dulaire shook her pretty head in protest.

I frowned. "I understand."

"Earl is a fine fellow by me." Mr. Dulaire frowned. "I think he can make Charlene happy. I don't think the same is true for you."

I heard Charlene come pounding down the front stairs in a soft steady beat. I saw her glance at herself in the long hallway mirror and stick out her tongue at the reflection and skip on out toward the front door, frowning once she saw me and her old man squared off.

"Daddy, what's going on?"

"Nothing, pumpkin. Me and Luce just having a little talk. Isn't that right, Luce? I think I made myself clear."

"Yes, sir, you have."

I turned and strode down their cement walk and out into the street. Charlene didn't come chasing after me. The thick white door closed as I turned the corner and crossed the street. There was no way I was good enough for that girl and I knew it. I had no business knocking upon her door and upsetting her folks and trying to prove that I was something better than I was.

This was a feeling no Ferris wheel or goldfish toss or snow-cone in a thin paper cup could ever hope to fix. But me and Junior went on to the Corn Fair anyway. He said it would be good for a fool with a broken heart like me. Hell, ol' Clutch was nice enough to let us close the gas station early so we could attend the festivities.

Then there was the Corn King and Queen. It was something like being in the homecoming or prom court. Two kids from the high school would be picked as the Corn King and Queen and got to ride on horseback through the town's streets at the head of the Corn Parade, which generally consisted of the two squad cars in town, the three fire trucks, the mayor's car, and some turn-of-the-century farm equipment driving down the main street to the tiny fairgrounds where the Corn Fair was always held.

"This is pitiful." I frowned.

I ate some cotton candy as me and Junior walked through the fair. It was a nice night out. People were talking loud and laughing and some Dixie band was playing "Oh When the Saints" on a little wood bandstand and the Ferris wheel was spinning around and some farmers were looking at a red 1923 tractor some other farmer had rebuilt. Most people I didn't seem to recognize, most people didn't seem to recognize me either, and that was fine. We saw Clutch getting drunk in the little beer garden and L.B. was following some poor girls around, and there was all the people I had ever sold gasoline to, smiling and laughing and having the time of their lives.

"This is pitiful all right." I frowned.

"C'mon, cheer up." Junior smiled. "You must know plenty of girls here in town."

"Know 'em, sure. But they haven't got what I already got in a girl that's too good for me."

Junior shook his head and handed me some more pink cotton candy, tearing it from the white paper cone. He looked happy. For once in a long time, he looked like he was having a nice time.

"That's not true, pal. You're as good a guy as I've ever met. If it wasn't for her folks, she might be here with you right now."

"If it wasn't for her folks, she probably woulda never stooped so low to date me in the first place. She probably dated me to give her lousy old man a heart attack, I bet."

We walked to the center of the fairgrounds and stopped where the Corn King and Queen were standing and smiling and waving and wholeheartedly greeting everyone in town to this year's Corn Fair. The Corn King was a pretty scrawny-looking kid with a big tuft of blond hair on his head and a dull look in his eyes and a huge horseshoe-shaped scar burned right on his left cheek. The kid's name was Young Benny Bilk. He was the state's all-around horseback riding champion for that particular year, but not much of a good-looking kid at that. He looked like he had been thrown or kicked in the head one too many times. He just kind of stood there and waved and mumbled hopelessly to himself.

Then there was the Corn Queen and her hair. It was like a little spell floated from her lips in each breath she exhaled. This girl was all the things that were good about that town, wrapped up in a puffy cornflower-blue dress and glass crown and her mother's shiny high heels. The most remarkable thing about this girl was her hair. It stood straight up, full of pomade and waves upon waves of hair spray. It brought a smile right to my face seeing that girl, standing there waving and smiling and winking like a queen. If one bead of sweat was running down along her spine, she wouldn't have let a single soul know. *Hope.* That's what that girl had. Hope that she was as true as the whole town believed.

Then a strange thing took place.

The snow-cone machine blew its silvery metal lid and shot right out from under its white tent and headed straight up into the sky like a kind of rocket ship, crashing into a bright white spotlight and smashing the fixture with a tremendous clatter that made the whole fair suddenly dull and still. Then it all rained down like a quiet little flight of snow and tiny bits of glass and ice, shimmering in the lights cast down by the Ferris wheel that kept spinning around, right past the bingo caller's noise, down into the Corn Queen's lovely red hair, where it sparkled like a single veil of fallen stars in place. It was beautiful. It was one of the most amazing things I'd ever seen. This girl just kept smiling and waving, blowing kisses everywhere as the night and the stars seemed to blossom up right in her thick red hair.

"She's beautiful." Junior smiled. "This town isn't half as bad as you said."

"I guess." I frowned. Junior passed me some more cotton candy and I swallowed it down and looked up into the stars right at the tip of that Ferris wheel. "I wish Charlene was here."

"Taking this awful hard, Luce. I thought you didn't like the idea of settling on down with just one girl yet."

"What the hell do I know? I mean, I keep thinking, what if she's the one for me?"

Junior shrugged his shoulders, then leaned in close with a big wide smile.

"Why don't you go and ask her for yourself?"

He gave a little nod and I followed his line of sight across the fairgrounds.

Charlene, all done up in a nice white blouse and a blue skirt that ruffled between her long white legs.

"What the hell should I do?" I mumbled.

"Go on off with her." Junior grinned.

"What about you? I ain't gonna leave you here by yourself."

"I've gotta open tomorrow anyways. You've been talking about her all night. Go on now and don't screw it up by being stubborn." He patted me on the back and gave a big smile as I took off.

I met Charlene right by the broken snow-cone machine. She gave a little smile then a frown when she caught sight of me.

"Didn't think you were planning on coming tonight," she said.

"Thought I might meet some girl who didn't have such a crazy old man."

"Well, good luck." She frowned and began to walk away.

"Wait a minute," I mumbled, grabbing for her hand. "Just wait a second. I was just kidding is all."

"I wouldn't blame you if you were looking to meet some other girl. I can't change the way my daddy is. It's lucky he didn't try to strangle you."

"That's funny," I said. "So you think your old man's right, huh? You think you're a little too good for me?"

"No." She frowned. "But you seem to."

She was right. She had showed up at the fair, knowing I would be there waiting to see her.

"Do you wanna go on a ride or something?" I asked.

"With you? In front of the whole town? What would everyone say?" She smiled.

"I couldn't give a damn."

"It's about time."

Charlene and I walked over to the shiny silver-and-white Ferris wheel and got right in line. This carnie with a red beard and a black patch over his eye took our tickets and locked us in place tight and threw the switch and sent us spinning up and around together right under that dull blue night.

Charlene moved closer to me and rested her head on my shoulder. It made me feel weak as hell, spinning around like that, smelling her hair. Then she slipped her tiny hand into mine and held on. Everything was perfect.

Charlene lifted her head a little and looked me in the eyes and gave a little frown. "How long do you plan on staying, Luce?"

"What's that?" I asked, still holding her hand tight as I could.

"How long do you plan on staying in town? Until your parole is served? Until you save up enough money to move out?" The silver-and-white lights flashed on by. Then big-brown-eyed Charlene looked away. "Until you're bored with me?"

I held her hand tight in my hand and shook my head. "Why are you talking like that now? What brought this all on?"

"You know what brought this on. My daddy and you arguing. I just want to be sure he isn't right."

"Isn't right? What do you mean?" I let go of her hand and shook my head.

"I mean, what are your plans? Do you want to work at that gas station forever? Do you want to stay in this measly town the rest of your life? What do you want to do with yourself?"

"I dunno." I frowned. "Maybe pick up a trade. I can fix some cars now, I guess. I could get a trucking license maybe. I really don't know. I never even thought about it until now. I was just happy sitting here holding your hand."

"Dammit, Luce, that's what I mean. You just don't seem to care. You don't seem to want the things I want at all."

"Like what, Charlene?"

"Well, I want to get out of this town for sure. Maybe go out West and go to beauty school and learn to do makeup for movie stars. But I know I'm getting out. I know one day I'll be married and have some kids and a nice little house and be settled down somewhere else, somewhere far away from here."

"Why do you hate this place so much?" I asked. "What did ol' La Harpie ever do to you?"

"Nothing." She frowned. "That's exactly the problem. You can't step outside your own house without hearing your neighbors talk about a rumor one of them heard about you. That's why I hate this town. Look at them. Look at them right now, all watching us."

I peered down from the Ferris wheel and gave a smug little grin. Charlene was right. Every busybody in town was watching the lowly ex-con and the daughter of the Used Car King holding hands and sitting close. All their dull eyes flickering along our skin, hoping to see us make some foul unrepentant mistake.

"Take your hand and put it on my heart," Charlene whispered. The soft timbre of her voice nearly made me blush. I nodded and placed my palm along her soft white blouse.

"Now kiss me," Charlene said, nodding with a grin.

"What?" I mumbled. "Right here?"

"Right here."

I nodded and gave her the kiss of my life. The Ferris wheel spun on down and around and the carnie with the red beard and eyepatch let us out and we walked right out of that fair, holding hands and laughing at the way everyone seemed to stare at us. We hopped in Charlene's car and drove away and then parked down the street from her house a little ways and began kissing and petting and getting sweaty in her backseat, mumbling to each other and still giggling like kids all right.

Afterwards, Charlene tendered a gentle kiss upon my lips, then turned and walked up to her house.

I thought for a minute that I was still back in the pen and this was all a kind of dream, but then I knew it was true.

strange customer

This place where I worked could be as strange and unpredictable as a night out kissing Charlene. Most of the time it was pretty dull and quiet. People usually just came in and filled their cars up and paid for their gas. But other times that gas station might be lurid and mean.

It all started with a bird.

I had been involved with a big 350-cid V-8 engine in a most personal way. Those sweet silver cylinders had me pulled in right down to their fiery pistons locked in place on a glossy magazine page.

Then a black bird hit the front glass window. It knocked me right out of my daydreaming during the middle part of my shift.

BOOM!!!

I snapped right awake.

The bird hit the glass and disappeared, dropping down into the dirt. It was one of those big black crows that ate all the dead things that drifted along the side of the road, this big black crow just plowed straight into the front glass window there and snapped its feathery neck and fluttered and twitched in place, *caw-caw-cawing* and hissing where it had bounced off the shiny glass. Then it landed and became silent and still in the dusty gray dirt.

There was no mark that it had smacked the glass except for a single spot where the damn thing's beak had hit. I looked out the window and stared at the spot and caught a glimpse of Junior's sign all in the same wink.

Fuel-line cleaner
on special
do shine
here thru
munificent dirt

I hopped from behind the counter and stepped outside. There it was, all puffed up and broken and bent, with its thick black wings fluttering and trembling in place, pounding its head against the dusty gravel as a line of blood dripped from its open beak.

CAW-CAW-CAW!!! it howled, pounding its thick little head against the ground. *CAW-CAW-CAW!!!* Its wings twisted up together one last time, in a kind of mockery of flight, then it fell still and collapsed on its side, breathing heavily, then lightly, then not at all.

I took all this to be a bad sign, and once I was sure it was dead and the first fly had landed upon the bird's open eye, I picked it up by its one broken wing and dropped it out back in the trash, gritting my teeth. I went back inside and washed my hands and stared at the shiny spot on the window.

A prostitute came in like a bad dream. It was the woman I had paid to make it with the first night I spent in town. She looked skinny and long and steady, and stunk of a desperate kind of perfume.

Then there was this sound. This sound she kept making. It rose right from her chest, a jerking kind of sound, like one of the valves of her heart was loose. It was the sound of something running on down. Trapped. Her heart gave another little start as she spoke and asked for a pack of smokes, leaning against the counter with a sigh and a low broken cough. She looked sick. She made me sorry for all the things I had ever dreamt or done to any girl I had ever known.

"Pack of Reds, Johnny," she murmured, letting all the jewelry and bracelets and bangles along her long thin arm dangle as she leaned against the counter.

I pulled the pack of smokes from the cigarette stock and placed it on the counter with a little smile.

She smiled back. "Hey, I know you, don't I, cream puff? I mean, you and I hit the hay once or twice, eh?"

Her cold blue eyes circled around inside her head as she tried to stare at me straight.

"Just once," I nodded, looking down at my hands. My face felt red all of a sudden and hot as hell. This girl looked bad. She looked old and tired and sick and torn apart by the things she had seen and done to herself.

"Was I worth your while?" she asked, giving a little smile.

"Sure." I tried to grin. "Everything was fine. It was nice all right. You're . . . very nice."

"Feel like having another nice time?" she murmured without any kind of sincerity.

"Not today." I frowned. "But thanks for asking."

"*Thanks for asking?* What do you think it is I'm giving away? Tickets to the parade?" She smiled again, making the jerking sound in her chest rise. *Thump-thump—thump-thump*, it muttered, tightening in place. "I got everything you want right here."

She leaned in close and made a little kissing movement with her worn-out lips. "I just need some money is all. I'm not asking for any handout, I'm willing to give you what you want and all."

"Here, listen, what's your name?" I asked, trying not to stare at her worn-out face.

"Tallulah." She frowned.

"It's a pretty name." I smiled. "It's a very pretty name." I dug into the back of my pants and took out my wallet and placed twenty bucks in Tallulah's hand. "Why don't you take this and get out of town? Why don't you take this and get on out and don't ever look back?"

Tallulah smiled and shook her head. "You don't understand. It's not like that at all. This is all my fault. This is all my own fault."

I stared at this girl, unable to speak.

Tallulah dropped some change and a dollar bill on the counter and placed the pack of cigarettes next to her heart.

"Don't go on thinking you ruined me," she whispered. "I did all these things myself. I did all these things without anyone else's help."

This lady turned and walked out of the store slowly, wobbling a little as one of her red high heels gave. She strode out through the glass doors, trying to light a cigarette and mutter to herself at the same time. It doesn't always work. Your hands sometimes shake too hard. This lady must have been a pro at it though. She lit the square on her first try and tossed the match into the dust, then walked on off.

I put the lady's change in the cash register and stared out those shiny glass windows some more.

BOOM.

Another bird hit the glass a few minutes later with a gentle kind of crash, more solemn and serious than the one before.

A little brown robin redbreast had slammed into the window, then fluttered on back, then slammed into the window again. The glass must have been too clean. It must have been too shiny and ended up reflecting the whole sky in its panes. I left the little spattering of blood where it had drawn cold. This time I didn't go on outside. I stood behind the counter where I was.

Some more customers came in, the dusk turned straight into night, dark and lonely and without a word or reply as I stared on out through those glass windows, sure that robin out there was lying in the dirt dead. I went up to the window and looked out and didn't see it lying there. It was gone. It had flown away. I went outside and looked for it all withered up in a corner somewhere but I couldn't find it. It was gone. I went back inside and thought about it all. I paged through some nudie magazines and helped myself to a pack of gum, and then, from out of the long, solemn, silent darkness of the night, two huge headlights burned on through and pulled up to the diesel pump, shining brightly along my eyes and face.

It was Guy Gladly. I saw his name written there in bright yellow letters along the side of his sturdy red rig. He left his truck idling and hopped on out and walked right through those double glass doors with a great big smile.

"Luce Lemay!" he shouted. "You doggone fool! How have you been, you doggone fool?!!"

He shook my hand hard with his big smile beaming, pushing back the nice black Stetson that sat atop his head. He had a square face and black mustache that curled up a little at its ends.

"Fine, Guy. I'm glad to say I'm doing fine."

"Well, hell's bells, you are a sight. Standing there like a decent citizen in your work clothes minding the store. You look upright, Luce. Like a regular Joe."

"Thank you." I grinned. "I do try."

Guy Gladly was a fine man by me. But not so much by the state police. I had met him in Pontiac, where he had been serving a five-year sentence for running stolen goods from town to town in the back of his beautiful long red rig. He was mostly gloomy and sullen during the time I had known him there. All he could talk about was missing his rig. Then he'd shake his head and spit at the floor like it hurt him to even breathe a breath that was filtered through those prison walls.

"Guy Gladly, what are you doing here?"

"Just passing through on my route. Thought I'd come by and see you. See how the jailbird's singing out of its roost."

He shook my hand again and punched me in the arm.

"God, man, it's good to see you. Seeing you here on the outside here, it's a real kick. It's a real, honest-to-goodness kick. So how's it feel?" he asked. "How's it feel to be free?"

"It's great." I smiled. "Don't feel much different myself, but it's all right."

"Give it a chance. Takes a little while to get back into step. You'll see, pal. You'll see."

He shook my hand again and gave a shout. Then he looked at me standing there all silent and still and gave a kind of half-cocked frown.

"Man, aren't you happy to be out? Aren't you happy to be a free man of your own?"

"Don't feel like it much right now, I guess." I frowned.

"What do ya mean? You're making your own way now. Living in your own bed, in your own place, got a real job, got more than thirty bucks in your pocket, huh? Living the way you wanna live, right? Heck, boy, you're freer than most men. Most men don't know what they got till they lose it. But you already know. You already know what it's like to be trapped in a little box. But now you're out! You're out on your own and free to start living your life again!"

Freedom had done wonders for Guy Gladly's disposition. This man used to sulk all around that lonely ol' prison, muttering to himself, shaking his head, even crying late at night. Now he was a changed man. Now he was saved by the wide black-and-yellow lanes of the interstate.

"I'm telling you, pal, I've got me a job again. Got back with my wife and we've got a little rug rat running around tearing things up. Got a nice little house and a little yard to lie in and a rig of my own. I'm living life on my own. That's what counts. Living the way I want. I don't give a damn about what some correctional officer thinks. That's what it's all about."

He nodded, agreeing with himself.

I smiled a little, shaking my head. "Guess I just don't feel like that."

"What's the matter with you, pal? We used to just sit around and talk about what we were gonna do as soon as we got out. What happened to all the things you wanted to do, pal?"

"Still feeling kinda trapped is all." I smiled.

"Well, jeez, Luce, the whole world don't end at the edge of this town. You need to move on, pal." He patted me on the shoulder and winked. "I brought something for you." He dug into his back pocket and pulled out something sweet. A beautiful silver harmonica. It was tiny and thin and shined like it was brand spanking new.

I began to grin right away.

"That the right kind?" Guy asked, sliding it across the counter with a smile.

"Sure is," I nodded. It said "*Horner*" along the top and bottom and the reeds inside still smelled like wood.

"That's the kind you like, ain't it?"

"You bet. You bet."

Someone had smuggled a harmonica into the pen and I spent all my cash on it and only got to play three songs before a C.O. took it away.

"How 'bout playing a little tune?" Guy asked, adjusting his black hat. "How 'bout something that cooks?"

I picked up the harmonica and placed it against my lips. I put

my tongue in place against the fourth hole and breathed in
through my nose. Then I broke on out. I broke on out through
"Alabama Moon" and "Countryside Blues" and kept blowing that
harp until my lips felt sore and hot, and then I played "Down by
the River" and "Little Red Rooster" until all the spit was gone in
my mouth and I was sure ol' Guy had about stamped a hole in the
goddamn tile floor.

"Ye-haw!" Guy shouted. "Now that's what it's all about.
Blowing those blues on out. Blowing them out."

I cleaned off the harmonica with my shirtsleeve and handed it
back to him.

"No, pal, that's yours. Keep you busy here at work."

He smiled and looked out the glass windows at the fading
lights of his truck. He saw Junior's garbled sign and gave a little
frown.

"How's old Junior anyway? He doin' all right?"

"Same, I guess. Still pretty gloomy himself," I said.

"You gotta watch out for him, Luce. You gotta make sure he's
on the straight and narrow. Make sure he's adjusting. Hate to find
out he hung himself or something sick like that."

"He's coming around, I think. I think he just needs a little
time."

"Sure, sure, pal. You, too. You, too. Three years or ten, going
from that place to the open world is a big change. A big change.
Not too many cons make it out here, do they? Gotta stick together,
I say. Stick together like horse glue." He looked at me again and
gave another big smile. "Good seeing you, Luce. Stand tall, convict. Stand tall."

He gave me a little wave and strode on out, back to his rig and
back into the open night. I put that harmonica up to my lips and
played "Dixie Blues" or as much as I could, forgetting a few notes,
stumbling some at the end, letting sweat gather just above my

mouth. It made me feel like the last lost few years of my life had only been a singularly long bad dream and this was the beginning— yep, this was the start of something bright and new and clean.

Then three more birds struck the glass and I wasn't so sure of anything.

Three yellow sparrows hit the glass all at the same time and dropped down into the dirt, flickering and fluttering full of blood and dust. This time I stepped outside. I stepped outside and stared at all three of them, lying there, chirping and crying and bleeding in the mud.

They were all so small. Their little eyes and mouths opened and closed. They were all still alive. They were all still alive and stuck on their backs with their broken wings spread beside them like little feathered coats, unbuttoned where they laid.

I turned away and went inside the gas station and grabbed the .22 that was hidden behind the counter and stood over those dying birds. I raised the gun, ready to fire, ready to put an end to all their voices, all their squalor and song.

But I didn't shoot.

Their singing had stopped.

I held that gun tight in my hands but didn't shoot. I felt like every damn thing in my life had hinged on those birds pulling through and now it was all about to take a turn for the worse.

I put the gun in the back of my pants. I locked the front glass doors and went around behind the Gas-N-Go to make a little grave for them in the soft gray dirt Clutch had tried to plant flowers in a few weeks before. Nothing had come up. None of the flowers Clutch had planted had even broke the dirt. I dug a hole, pretty tiny but as deep as I could, and walked around to the front again to collect the birds. Just as I hunched over to scoop one of them up, a nice black Cadillac Fleetwood pulled into the parking lot, pulled to a complete stop, then sped up, right past the pumps,

and stopped a few feet from where I was kneeling. The driver's
door opened and two feet in black snakeskin cowboys boots and
silver spurs stepped on out, and before I could turn all the way
around I heard a voice, a timbre so bare and soft, echo right in my
ear and chest.

> *"Mi corazon de luce*
> *esta muerto y perdido*
> *mas alla de mí*
> *mas alla de tu*
> *cerca de los Dios y las estrellas*
> *cerca de la verdad . . ."*

I looked on up and began to sweat.
It was Toreador. He was breathing right in my ear.
He looked right into my eyes and smiled a wee little smile.
"Hello, my motherfucker. How is everything down there?"
He lifted back his fist and hit me with all five knuckles right
along my chin. Then it all went black. It all went black and red.
"Didn't think you'd see me again, eh?" he hollered, kicking my
chin, cracking me where my shoulder met my neck along the side
of my throat. My head was throbbing full of loose blood. I could
feel it running down the side of my lip. I couldn't get up. I couldn't
get up to stand. He had me by the front of my shirt. He had my
hand pinned along the ground. Then he pulled a small black-
handled knife from the side of his belt. Toreador placed the knife's
edge against my face and cut, running along the side of my face
slowly, slicing my cheek in a thin shallow graze.
"There you go, cholo." He grinned. "Now you're pretty as me."
I went for the .22 in the back of my pants but the bastard
stood on my hand with his shiny black boot. He put the knife
against my eye and grinned.

"Old Jimmy Fargo said he saw you get off in this town." Toreador smiled. "Then I checked with my boys inside and they said you got a job working here. I drove all the way down here from Chicago just to see you tonight, Luce. Just so you could pay me back for the scar those C.O.'s gave me. Look at this!" he shouted. "Look what those fuckers did to my face."

I looked up from the dirt and the mud right at his cheek and saw a long puffy red scar that ran from the corner of his thin gray lips to his deep black eye.

"We're gonna go inside and empty out your cash drawer, then go for a little ride." He grinned, holding the knife over me.

I couldn't breathe. The pain in my neck had me paralyzed, down on my knees.

"Get to your feet, cholo." Toreador still grinned. But I didn't move. My body was all cramped up in agony. "Come on, cocksucker, get to your feet."

I closed my eyes and grabbed a handful of gravel and dirt and leaned back on my legs and threw it all as hard as I could right into that bastard's face.

"Cabrón!" he howled, covering his face. Then I pulled the gun from the back of my pants and slammed it hard into his throat. He froze. He froze where he stood and then I cracked him with the butt of the .22 against his face, catching him right under his goddamn chin. He flew back with a grunt against the front of his car, then pulled himself to his feet. I lunged forward and slammed the gun into his face again, pinning his wrist against the hood of the car with my other hand until his knife slipped out and dropped into the dirt. He slumped to the ground, holding the blood on his chin with his fingers, still smiling like a lunatic.

"Go on, cholo, finish me off," he hissed.

"I ain't a goddamn killer like you . . ." I muttered. "I ain't a goddamn killer like you . . ."

"Sure you ain't, cholo." He grinned through some spit. "You just keep saying it to yourself and maybe you believe it, eh?"

I squeezed the pistol hard, maybe hoping to blow off his goddamn head, but I blew out his headlight instead and placed the warm muzzle against his teeth.

"Don't come back here . . ." I grunted. "Don't ever come back again . . ."

"I don't need to. Now you think about me every time you look at your lousy face, eh? Now you can't think about being pretty without thinking about me."

"Get out!!" I shouted, and slammed him up against his steely silver grill. Toreador nodded and pulled himself to his feet and wobbled back into his car and drove away, still grinning like a lunatic, still staring at me until he had disappeared back into the night. I fell against the glass doors and tumbled inside.

I managed to lock the front doors and fall behind the counter before blacking out again.

My cheek was bleeding like crazy now. I held a rag against the side of my face and had my head down on the counter, staring outside into the darkness, mumbling to myself. It was all too much. The planet had moved backwards and then ahead again too quick. It all didn't make sense. It had all moved too fast.

I held the rag to my face and walked outside and locked the front doors and stared down at those three birds in the dust and gray and dirt. I picked them all up, I picked all three of them up, and held them to my cool blue work shirt and went around back and placed them in that shallow little hole. I swept a thin wake of soft black dirt over their thinned yellow feathers, all bent out of place, their hollowed eyes and crescent-shaped beaks, I spread the dirt over them all and buried them there to rest.

The blood on my cheek had gone dark and red and had stopped running, growing thick and smooth where I had been cut.

I rubbed my dirty hands on my pants and went back inside the Gas-N-Go and shut off all the lights and locked it up good. Then I stumbled the few blocks in the dark to the Starlite Diner and stood outside of it, staring at it all lit up. There was Charlene behind the counter, pouring a cup of joe for some old trucker, smiling, pushing her hair over her shoulder in the nicest way a man like me could ever imagine it being done. I stood out there alone in the dark, feeling that cut on my face, feeling my legs buckling at my knees from the pain in my head and my throat and my cheek, still spitting gravel from out of my teeth, and I felt something there.

It was a little prayer of a girl serving coffee, standing there with all my hope laid upon her hands like a white piece of cake. Suddenly I knew where I was and where I was going and who might be beside me when I got there. A single word came upon my lips and I wanted to sing it in a little whisper, in a little song to make her hear, to make her see, but my lips were too sore and my throat was too weak and the only tune I could hear was that word. It kept me on my feet until I found my bed, and even then, even then, there was a little whisper of it left to follow me off to sleep and some sound, sound dreams of my own quiet and unresonant kind of reprieve.

Good night . . . the quiet room said around me.

Good night . . . it all seemed to whisper songlike to me.

long black veil

For a whole week I found myself lying wide awake, unable to fall back asleep, listening to a gentle-throated moaning all alone in the night. I had heard someone calling out there in the dark myself for eight nights straight. At first I thought it was Junior in there muttering or crying to himself, but it wasn't coming from his room. It was coming from the hall. From outside the door. I thought I was maybe losing my mind.

I laid like that for eight nights, trying to decide what to do. Finally, I got up enough courage to pry myself out of bed to take a look. I didn't know if I was more afraid I'd see something out there that was some kind of spook or specter, some kind of figment of my lonely imagination, or that I wouldn't see anything at all, and then that would mean I was crazy and past any kind of any hope.

I placed my bare feet along the cold wood floor, stepping lightly, holding in my breath as I listened to the gentle moan, reverberating right outside my door. I rubbed the sleep out of my eyes and put my hand along the gold doorknob and gave it a slow, careful turn, sure not to make any sound, feeling my heart beginning to beat somewhere within my throat. There it was. I could hear it again. A voice, calm and lilting and sweet, echoing right down the hall. I turned the doorknob, then pulled the door open.

There was a shadow out there. It moved along the hallway wall in slow, regretful steps. It crept closer, closer, the moaning growing louder and louder as it moved. I sucked in a breath through my teeth and was closing the door when a thin gray hand reached out to me, cold as the grave. What I had found was much more startling than any delusion or bad dream.

It was Old Lady St. Francis all dressed up in proper funeral clothes, complete with black dress and long black gloves, a black purse, and a black veil covering her elderly face.

"All wounds do not heal . . ." she whispered, holding my wrist tight. "All wounds do not mend so easily . . ."

"I reckon not," I whispered in reply. She let go of my wrist, then began to walk down the hall again, moaning through her black veil. I shook my head and went back inside the room and pulled on my pants and followed her down the hall, hoping to maybe steer her back to her room at the foot of the staircase.

"Forgive me, but it seems you're not properly dressed," she said in a kind little smile. "That's no way to show respect for the dead," she said, staring at my dirty blue work pants smudged with grease stains.

"I'm sorry." I smiled. "I didn't know I'd be going anywhere tonight."

Then she said it again.

"All wounds do not heal . . ." She coughed. "Old wounds do not heal so easily . . ."

"We need to get you back in bed."

"Trick-trick-trick, the walls begin to drip. Thick as blood on your lips. Trick-trick-trick."

"That's fine, sweetheart. How about going back to bed?"

"OK."

She put her hand in mine and we began to make our way

down the darkly lit red-carpeted stairs. I could see the outline of
her face behind the veil. I could see her lips and the tip of her nose
and her eyes, pale blue and huge and burning bright. She looked
drugged, like she was walking in some kind of dream.

"Have you ever ridden in a limousine?" she asked me.

"Nope." I smiled, helping her down the first flight, careful not
to hold her thin little hand too tight.

"It was long and black and shined like marble. It was the prettiest car you could imagine. It took us all the way around town
and through the streets and back past the church where we got
married and then down La Harpie Road and out to the cemetery
and then it began to rain and Mr. Wallace, the director, was afraid
I was going to catch my death standing there like that, but I didn't
mind. I needed to be there. They were both there, lying two rows
apart. My husband and Ben Veree in their casket boxes. They put
my husband in the ground and I knew he didn't mind sharing
space with Ben. His wife wouldn't let me see him before they laid
him to rest. That was OK. I understood her pain. But at least our
husbands were buried close. They were the best of friends their
whole life, and that's not a thing that's likely to change in death."

I nodded, holding her soft, wrinkled hand in mine.

"Here we go, sweetie." I smiled, reaching her red wood door.
"Here we are. Back to bed."

"Lay to waste," she mumbled. "Lay in waste. It doesn't make
sense, does it? It doesn't seem fair to lose both the men I loved."

"No, it doesn't. It doesn't seem fair at all."

"Mr. Wallace, will you take me to the cemetery tomorrow? I'd
like to visit their graves and make sure they're doing OK."

"Sure." I smiled, knowing this would all be some kind of
strange dream to me by the morning. "Sure. That sounds fine."

"Good night," she whispered, and laid down on her bed.

I closed her door quietly and crept back up the stairs, shaking my head, muttering to myself. I fell back into my bed and gave a little prayer that she would soon be back asleep and forget it all by morning, that she'd be too mean and proud to ask me to escort her out there to the graveyard.

I must have put my prayer in too late.

She knocked at my damn door at a quarter to seven in the morning, dressed in the same black dress, black gloves, black purse, and veil.

"Good morning," she whispered. That was it. That's all she said. The blue look had left her eyes but she was somehow still the same. I gave a little cough and cleared my throat and tried to think of something to say. It was Sunday morning. The day of rest. I had to go to work at two and had planned on sleeping in until then. But now it was too late. This lady was all ready to go. She had picked two big bouquets of bright yellow daffodils from her yard and was standing outside my door, staring at me quietly through that veil.

"Just one second." I tried to smile. "Just let me get dressed."

I put on my cleanest shirt and red suit coat and red pants and combed my hair and washed my face and met her at the bottom of the stairs, trying to think of something to say. But nothing would come. Somehow, I expected her to be mean. But she wasn't. She was just quiet. Even after she started walking toward the bus stop and when we got to the end of the street, she just put her arm in mine very gently and allowed me to help her cross. Then she kept it there, placing her thin gray hand along my arm, leaning against me as if she was suddenly a lot older and much more weak. She had lost something in her life, two men, two men she might have loved very much, all on her own account.

"The bus frightens me sometimes." She smiled, showing her tiny little teeth. "Sometimes I'm afraid I might get on the wrong one and not know where I am, so I let it go on sometimes and sometimes I wait for the next one, or the one after that."

In her voice was all the weight of her life.

"There was no showdown or anything deliberate like that. Poor Willem found me there in our bed, not alone, not by myself, and went downstairs and got his gun and came back and shot poor Ben in the head and then placed the gun against his nose and pulled the trigger once more. I ran out of the house in my night-clothes and hid under the porch out back, and when the sheriff came and found me, they said there were pieces of Ben's scalp and Willem's blood all stuck together in my hair."

I felt my mouth become a hollow little hole.

"Ben's wife came over and broke out all the windows in the house, then she collapsed on the front porch and I ended up holding her in my arms all night, crying together like that, then that was it and I never talked to her or saw her again," she muttered, crossing her hands. "I haven't been here in twelve years," she whispered. "Not since my niece, Julee, left town."

We got off the bus at the cemetery gates and I helped her down as she held my arm tight.

The gates rose like a grave of their own, locking you in a place of slumber and rest. We stepped along the thin path until that ended and there was nothing but an expanse of dirt and grass and shiny gray gravestones that stretched right along this little hill. The founders of La Harpie had gotten something right. But not at first. They had built the cemetery on low land at first and after one spring when the river thawed and rose and flooded the town, it swept away some of the graves and deceased and replanted them somewhere closer to Mississippi. They moved the rest of the bodies up the hill, out of harm's reach, surrounding the graveyard with a thick wood fence and iron gate that had begun to wear from the cold winter and sleepy rains. It looked like a place that might just suddenly crumble apart into dust.

"They're never too far away . . ." she whispered, holding my hand tight. "Never too far away."

We walked a little ways toward the center of the cemetery and then she stopped and let go of my arm and laid one of the yellow bouquets beside Benjamin Veree's shiny black grave. She nodded to herself, then walked on a little more and stopped in front of Willem Tany's headstone, holding the flowers to her chest.

"Here he is," she muttered, holding her hand up to her face. "Here he is asleep . . ."

I nodded and placed my hand on her tiny shoulder and stared hard at that shiny black grave. *Willem Tany.* It was all there. A clean little life left in a few simple names and dates.

"Even the dirt looks like it's asleep." She coughed, reaching up under her veil to wipe her eyes with the end of a blue flowered hanky. I held in my breath and took a step back, staring down at my feet.

"I'm sorry," she whispered, shaking her head. "I wasn't ready for this. I wasn't ready to see him like this . . ."

"It's fine, ma'am. Take all the time you need."

She nodded and turned her head and faced the clean stone slate. I took a few steps back and began to walk away. It struck me all at once. The ground felt like it shifted under my feet. There was something there I ought to go see. There was someone there waiting for me.

I stepped lightly along the grass, barely looking at the gravestones as I passed, trying to keep my eyes shut as far as I could manage. There was nothing there I wanted to see. There was nothing there I wanted to face. I kept looking for a very tiny one, one that rose shorter than the rest, one that looked completely out of place in a cold little acre of rest like that.

Hyacinth.

It wasn't there.

I couldn't find it. I couldn't remember her last name. That

wasn't true. I knew her last name as sure as the lines in my hand.
But I couldn't face that tiny cold stone.

Some wounds can't ever be healed.

Some wounds can't be turned away.

I went back and found Old Lady St. Francis clutching her
husband's grave, digging her thin white fingers into the stone,
moaning to herself as she let it all out. Then she stopped and was
still and quiet and took my hand and began to walk away. I could
understand. For her, it would never be done. It would be a thing
that would never be quite asleep.

We got back on the bus and she didn't say another word. She
didn't even make another sound until we were already walking
back to the hotel and she stopped and lifted her veil and tried to
turn her gray little lips into a thin little smile.

"Thank you," she mumbled. "It's not an easy thing for me to
do. Cry and burden myself on other people like that. Thank you
for that."

I squeezed her hand and helped her up the porch stairs, feeling her weight trembling upon my hand. She turned and smiled
again, a thin little feeble smile, and parted her lips like she wanted
to say something else but it was all OK. We had seen each other's
darkest waking dreams, and now there was nothing else that
needed to be said.

I sat on the back porch that afternoon and had a few bottles of
beer before work, then got changed and went off to the Gas-N-Go
for my shift. The night went by pretty quick and I was still in a
kind of somber, pensive mood, watching all the cars go by, switching their lights on as the dusk rolled into night, and it seemed that
whole Sunday was a kind of long church ceremony and everything
I did from staring out the window to mopping the floor to locking
the door was somehow holy. I looked forward to going back to the
hotel and sitting on the back porch or in Junior's room and seeing

his wide round face as a kind of relief. I made it home and went up to his room and couldn't find him there, so I walked back down the stairs and outside and saw him under the back porch, digging by himself in the dirt.

"What the hell are you doing under there?" I asked, patting him on the back. He looked up. His round face was smeared with dirt. He was hunched there on his hands and knees, gritting his teeth, his lips frozen in a frown that showed all of his pain.

"It changes," was all he mumbled back to me. "It changes everything."

I looked down and saw what he had dug. He had dug up that yellow cigar box with the tiny bird he had found beside his head. That yellow box rested gently in his hands, opened, buzzing with flies and the musty odor of decay. I covered my mouth and backed away, shaking my head.

"What the hell did you go and dig that thing up for?" I asked, staring at his sweaty face.

"It's some kind of magic," he muttered over his dirty lips. "It changes everything."

The tiny eyeless bird in the box was gone. Now there was just worms and hard-bellied insects and millipedes and dust and tiny grayed bones. There were some very thin feathers and its hard little feet twisted up tiny and thin, but it was no longer a bird, it no longer resembled anything that might have flown or breathed or lived or died. It was now something else. Something changed.

"I've been hearing things at night," he muttered. "I've been hearing things and I wanted to be sure. I wanted to be sure if a thing is dead it doesn't stay the same."

His eyes were big and blue and cold. He was serious all right. More serious and stern than I had ever seen him behave.

"It changes," he whispered, closing the cigar box. "It doesn't stay the same."

"It was the old lady," I mumbled. "It was her making those sounds at night."

Junior shook his head. "It doesn't stay the same after you're dead."

"But . . ."

"It wasn't her. It couldn't have been her because she wouldn't be the same."

His eyes lingered over the box as he set it back in the dirt. I nodded and went inside and up to my room and laid down on my bed.

I went outside and walked down the street and hitched on out to La Harpie Road. I stood right there not far from the highway where it all happened about three years ago in the middle of the night. I stood right in the middle of the road below the streetlamp that flickered green then yellow then red then green again in a message I couldn't quite understand. There was no marking there in the dirt or dust. No space left along the road that showed where that sweet young baby girl lost her life. I walked about a half-mile to Laverne Street and down to the end of the block. There was that baby's sweet white house. There was where her parents lived and mourned, nestled under a pretty black-tiled roof and white wood porch. I had come out here before the trial. I had stood right in front of the porch and then ran away. There were things in that house I couldn't face. Things that hung over my head with every breath I managed to take. But now it was all done. All just dirt in a yellow cigar box. I walked up the steps and knocked on the front door. A nice, round-faced lady answered the door.

"Is Mr. or Mrs. Heloise home?" I muttered in a quick breath.

"No, I'm sorry, they don't live here anymore. They must've moved out of here about three years ago or so."

I nodded, not saying a word.

"Lost their baby in an accident down the road. Terrible thing. They decided it was best to pick up and move. I still get mail for them sometimes. Sweet couple, they were. Sweet as a pea. Hate to see something tragic like that happen to nice people like that."

I nodded again, staring down at my shoes. The porch beneath my feet was still. The whole world was quiet tonight.

"Thanks."

"Were you an acquaintance of theirs?" she asked.

"Yes."

"Would you like to leave your name? If I hear from them anytime soon, I can tell them you stopped by."

"No, that's all right . . . I just came by to see how they were. Thanks," I mumbled. "Thanks again."

"Surely."

The nice lady smiled at me and closed the door. I stood out on the porch and held in my breath. I could feel my hands shaking at my side. I could feel my heart shaking inside. I stared at the blue and pink flowers in bloom that rose out of wooden boxes beside the door.

"I'm sorry," I whispered. "I'm sorry in a way I hope you might never know."

The buds remained still in their vase.

"I'd trade my life for yours right know, I swear to God. But I know wishing and dreaming like that doesn't do you any good. I'm sorry . . . I'm sorry . . . I wish I could say it all a better way . . ."

I stared at those flowers once more, then turned and walked down the porch steps and back out on the road.

lonely driver

Before the engine was even off, Charlene was tugging at her brassiere and had me pinned against the soft vinyl seat in a soft-lipped kiss. This was more than I could have hoped for. These moments between us were better than anything I could have ever wished.

"What happened to your cheek?" she asked, staring at me.

"I got hurt at work," I said, which was both a lie and not a lie.

"Thank God I don't like you for your looks," she joked.

"Thank God," I said.

"Take my bra in your mouth and pull," Charlene giggled, pressing her chest to my face. I shrugged my shoulders and removed it with my teeth. There was the smoothest softest plane of flesh I had ever seen. There was something there that lit a fire under all my skin, that made all my past disappear, that made me think I could do just about anything as long as she was close by.

Charlene managed to keep a permanent smile on my old tired face. Even when she wasn't beside me. Even when her sweet perfume wasn't in the air and her kiss wasn't close by.

Then there was a thing or two that felt kind of out of place about the whole blessed thing. Mostly, Earl Peet's sturdy white fists slamming into my teeth.

The Gas-N-Go gave me a minimal warning sign. I finished stocking the sundries and cookies and crackers shelf and hopped on back behind the counter, when the tiny silver bell above the door gave a little ring. I turned and stared right into Earl Peet's face.

"You've been with Charlene," Earl grunted, shaking his head. "I told you what would happen if you saw her again."

"Christ, Earl, she's a grown woman. She can see whoever the hell she wants to see."

"Naw, you got her all confused. She don't know if she's coming or going."

"I don't think Charlene would see it like that. I think she'd say something about you not knowing when something's over."

"That so?" Earl grinned, turning his loose fingers into steady white fists.

"Maybe not." I smiled. "Maybe I don't know her so well."

I began looking behind the counter for something to defend myself with. There was the old .22 stashed under the cash register drawer. But shooting him would only create more problems for myself, one of which would be the certain end of the romance between me and Charlene.

"Come on out from around that counter," Earl muttered, looking me hard in the eyes.

"Christ, Earl, we already seem to know how this is all gonna end. Mostly with more of my teeth on the floor. Don't you think we can settle this some other way?"

"No," Earl grunted. "Now come on out from behind there."

"I'm working here, Earl, I got a gas station to run. Can't you come back some other time?"

Earl lunged for me and grabbed hold of my blue work shirt, gripping it hard. Then he spat right in my goddamn face. There was something so sad, so pitiful stocked-up there in his eyes. Hurt, I guess.

"Now you come out and around before I tear you and this place all up."

I nodded, then reached for the pistol and shoved it right in his face. "Get the hell out of my store."

Earl didn't move at all. He stared right at me from over the barrel of the gun, looking at me hard with those cold black eyes, shaking his head real slow.

"I ain't afraid of dying, Luce Lemay. You should know that now. But you oughta be afraid to go anywhere without that goddamn gun."

"Get the hell out," I mumbled, still holding the gun to his forehead. "Don't come on back, either. We don't appreciate your business."

He stared at me hard once more, then turned and walked out through the double glass doors. He left behind a notion that this was the beginning of something worse.

It all hit me like a head-on collision as I walked on home alone, humming to calm myself. I saw the headlights coming from down the road.

There was nowhere to run. That road was long and straight and narrow, and as soon as I made for the shoulder I realized it was just as flat and plain as the highway itself.

I closed my eyes and the pickup's engine roared and then I felt the side of the front fender slam hard into the back of my left knee, knocking me clear off my feet. I rolled along my face and side of my head in the dust. The pickup braked and parked cockeyed along the road, and then sped off. I lay there a long while, holding my sore side, unable to move.

I made it on home and crashed through my door and fell beside my bed, hitting my head on the floor with my face. Then Junior came in right away and stood over me, mumbling something, lifting me up. All I could say was that intolerable name.

"Earl Peet." I coughed. "Earl Peet."

Junior helped me into my bed and laid a cold rag on my face and took off my shoes and closed the door and turned out the light. Then he grabbed his tools from his room and took a little walk all alone in the dark.

He was the best friend any man could have.

He placed the claw-hammer against that shiny silver door handle and pried it off, catching it in his huge white palm.

He put the ratchet against the bolt on the door and turned.

It began to come undone right in his own hands.

He went right to work and opened the door and slipped the gear into neutral, then gave that red pickup a push. He pushed it all the way out and down the street, then behind the Fleckens's woodshed way out in the back of their property, all alone, shaded by the weeping willows in the dark. Then he took it apart. He took the whole fucking thing apart. He worked all night, with the hammer and ratchet and wrench and his tools, then left a message in Earl Peet's yard using some black rubber hoses and part of the grill and some of the transmission and radiator parts and the muffler and some bent wheel rims. He left a message there in the dark using the oil from Earl Peet's red pickup truck, left it right along his gray driveway in huge black letters that fucker would be able to read.

HE
WITHOUT
SIN

When that bastard Earl stepped out of his yard to go to work, his whole face sunk right in and he fell to his knees, shaking his head.

"No," he whispered. His pretty red truck was gone. In the space where it had been parked there was nothing but torn-up truck parts.

I wish I could have seen his slack-jawed face.

It was right then, dreaming of Earl gawking at the truck parts on his lawn, that I was sure Junior Breen was the most loyal, truest man I would ever know. Hell, that big fool was on parole, too. But he hadn't cared. He had seen me, had done a thing for me without thinking. Without thinking, he had risked being sent back behind bars.

If anyone I knew deserved something sweet and true, it was him.

Three days later, it arrived. I stepped out of the Gas-N-Go and smiled, staring at one of the prettiest sights I had ever seen.

There was ol' Junior behind the wheel of the most beautiful car I could dream.

It was a big black Monte Carlo SS, maybe an '86 or '87, with the roaring 305 V8 and glasspacks underneath and huge silver rims, jacked up in the back like a real hot rod, kicking up dust and exhaust where it was parked between the Number 2 and Number 4 pumps.

"Sweet mother of God," I mumbled over my dry gums. "Now that is a goddamn car."

Junior just grinned and gunned the engine some more, listening to it growl like a jungle cat.

"How the hell did you afford that?" I asked.

"I didn't," he mumbled. "I'm taking it for a test ride."

"A test ride?"

"Sure, sure. Mr. Dulaire down there at the dealership let me take it for a spin."

"He let you take it for a spin?" I muttered.

"Told him I was new in town and just bought a farm a few miles away."

"You thinking of buying a car?"

"Nope." Junior smiled. "Just saw it sitting there on the lot and it reminded me of a car I wanted when I was seventeen."

"Hell yeah it does. This is the goddamn car every seventeen-year-old kid would want." I ran my hand along the smooth black hood, feeling it glisten under my skin.

"This car is prettier than most girls in town." I grinned.

"Sure is." Junior smiled. "Hey, do you wanna go for a ride?" he asked, revving the engine again.

"A ride . . . ?" I mumbled. "What about the gas station here?"

"Heck, ol' Clutch won't mind if you take a little break. Five minutes in the sweetest ride of your life."

I gave a little chuckle and pulled down my cap and stared at Junior there. Behind that wheel, he was a changed man. He was free. You could nearly see it in his face. His blue eyes were shining bright and his teeth were stuck together in the biggest smile I'd ever seen him make.

"Guess five minutes won't hurt," I said. I went back and locked up the front glass doors. Then I touched that car's silver handle and got on in and felt myself disappear right there.

Junior took it out on the highway and we tooled along, taking 101, spinning past all the farms and fields and barns out there, blowing past it all.

"This car is hell on wheels," I howled, holding my head out the passenger window. "It's a goddamn hell on wheels!"

Junior nodded and smiled warmly to himself. Then his eyes got dark and he mumbled something to himself.

"This is what it must feel like to be free."

We cut back down the highway and along La Harpie Road past the cemetery gates and those poor sleeping souls and then straight through downtown, the two of us fool ex-cons on parade in the most magnificent car of all time, driving past all the gawkers and needle-eyed gossipers with the biggest smiles either of us ever wore. Then Junior hit the gas and we were off again and back out on La Harpie Road heading toward the Gas-N-Go, and then he blew right past, past that beatific little filling station there like he was blowing right into the future, blowing alongside it all and straight ahead, the both of us moving fast.

This car was fast.

This car was maybe fast enough to outrun all of our pasts. Junior spun the car around and headed back.

"How much does this baby cost?" I shouted, leaping out in front of the Gas-N-Go as soon as Junior came to a stop.

"Too much." Junior frowned.

"Too much? How much? How much could it cost?"

"Five grand." He sulked.

"Five grand?! We can get five grand!"

"All I got is three," Junior mumbled. "I don't wanna wait another eight months to save up the rest of the cash."

"What about a loan?" I asked. "Maybe you could get one, huh?"

"Not with my record. Mr. Dulaire'll take a look at it and have himself a good laugh."

"Huh," I muttered. "Huh."

Then it hit me. "Hell, I've got a few hundred bucks. Maybe if we throw in and give him what we got now, he'll let us pay him the rest as we go."

Junior stared at me, then smiled.

"This is Charlene's old man, right?" he asked.

I nodded and spat in the dirt. "What about Clutch? Maybe he can spot us the rest and we can pay him back."

Junior looked at me and shrugged his shoulders. "Couldn't hurt to ask."

"That's all you'd have to do."

"You think?" Junior smiled.

"Sure as I'm standing staring at the prettiest car in the world."

It worked. Clutch lent ol' Junior and me the rest of the money and the three of us went down there to pick the car up. When god-damn Mr. Dulaire saw me standing there, he nearly dropped the shiny silver keys he was holding.

"What . . . you taking that car?" he mumbled, rubbing his thick greasy chin.

"Yes, sir." I smiled. "Maybe I'll come by and cruise past your house in it tonight."

Milford Dulaire kept his composure. He straightened his thick brown tie and handed Junior the keys and Clutch the regis-tration and all three of us howled and went outside and started that car up and drove, we just drove on and on until the sun had about set and then we went by the Gas-N-Go to fill that sweet car up again, and at about that time is when I noticed little Monte Slates, the kid who liked tossing water balloons down onto the interstate, sitting out beside the gas station there, crumpled up in a little ball, burying his face into his knees, hiding between a stack of used tires and some old cardboard cases of Valvoline and grease.

"Monte?" I mumbled, standing over him, trying to get a look at his face. "Monte, pal, you OK?"

He shook his head, still crying to himself. He stunk of dirt and sweat and that salty-sweet breath of tears.

"Monte, pal, you wanna talk? You come here to talk it out?"

He shook his head, still keeping his face buried beside his legs.

"Come on now, pal, look at me. You OK?" I asked.

He shook his head, then lifted his chin and I caught sight of something horrible on his face. There was a burn right on his cheek, the exact size of a cigarette tip, bright and red and blistered in his poor white skin. His face looked so old and round and sweet and his little cheeks shimmered with tears, slipping past that little burn.

A cigarette tip.

I gritted my teeth together and shook my head, turning my hands into hard fists at my side.

"He threw me out," Monte cried, his eyes burning red with tears. "Now I got no place to stay."

Junior and Clutch came up behind me and kept quiet, looking stern and serious and staring at the cigarette burn on poor Monte's face. They peered down at the boy, then at me, and then shook their heads slowly, trying not to let Monte see how pitiful, how small and sad his poor face seemed.

"It's gonna be OK," I mumbled, trying to think of something better to say. I placed my hand on his tiny shoulder and helped him to his feet. "It's gonna be OK, pal. You'll see. We're gonna take care of this right away."

Clutch took little Monte's hand and went over and unlocked the gas station and led him inside and treated him to a nice ice cream sandwich, patting him on the head once or twice, showing the poor kid his old faded tattoo, making that sweet island girl dance longingly as he moved his wrist.

Junior and I got inside that black car and drove right over to the Slates's place. It still looked rundown as hell. There were insects crawling around and the stink of dirt and ignorance seeping right out of the boards someone had used to build that white porch.

"What do you want to do?" Junior asked me, tightening his lips into a stern frown.

I wasn't really sure what he was asking. I knew what I was going to do. I walked up on that porch and pounded hard on their faded white front door. Then I heard him. I heard that weak little man wobble to the door, shifting his weight on his black-handled canes, pulling himself along like a broken ol' snake, until he was at the door and had it unlocked. He stuck his miserable gray face out and gritted his teeth, because he caught sight of me, because he saw the look in my eyes and the darkness in my own face. He didn't turn away. He didn't make a sound, just stood there looking back at me like I had just caught him doing something he shouldn't have ever done.

"Plea . . ." he muttered, but it was too late. I tore that god-damn door open and slammed my fist into his thin grayed face.

Junior stood over me as I slapped that fucker in his face with the flat of my palm, pinning him down against his dirty floor, slapping as hard as I could because hitting him with my fists might have left a bruise for poor Monte to see. His pink plastic feet struck together, hitting the floor with a hollow, unholy sound, like the teeth in my head were grinding together, like all the blood in my veins was coming apart.

"I warned you!!" I shouted. "I warned you to leave that boy alone!!"

Mr. Slates's face was beginning to swell around his thin gray lips, his sad yellow eyes were full of tears, he clutched at my shirt, trying to push me off as I slapped him again hard across his mouth. Then I wrapped my hands around his greasy little throat.

"Wait," Junior whispered. "Just wait." He pulled me off by my shoulder and backed me away. Mr. Slates lay still on the floor, wiping the blood from his teeth.

"Charity . . ." Junior whispered, shaking his head. "Charity . . ."

He went over and picked Mr. Slates up by the front of his oily blue flannel shirt, then dragged him into the kitchen and threw the bastard hard against the tiny white stove. Then he lit the range. The fire whispered bright blue along the black metal grate. Junior lit the stovetop and turned the gas on up until the flame burned there bright and blue and hot.

He turned to me, and suddenly I could see all the hard things he had ever felt lit up upon his face.

"I will put it right on his skin," Junior mumbled. "Make sure it is a word he doesn't forget."

He grabbed Mr. Slates's hand and pushed it toward the flame, holding it there as Mr. Slates began to howl and scream and struggle to try to get free, but Junior was too strong and too angry and too full of hate, hate for all the ignorance he had seen, hate for the ignorant things that had been done to people like him and Monte and even me. I just closed my eyes and turned away. I could hear Mr. Slates scream. I stood on the porch and watched as all the neighbors came out to see what was the trouble. Not one of them had noticed Monte's face? Not one of them had seen that boy sleeping outside, curled up in a ball underneath his dirty white front porch because his father had thrown him out? No, no, it was too hard to believe. Especially in this town.

Junior stepped out on the porch and nodded to me, and I looked back inside and saw Mr. Slates lying there on the floor, moaning and sobbing and holding his hand, and Junior glanced around and saw all the neighbors, blank-eyed and standing on their porches, staring at us and past us into the dirty white house, and he just shook his head and got into the black car and I followed and we pulled away, me feeling like we hadn't done a thing.

That fire spread from right outside the Slates's door and from those careless neighborhood eyes right across the hood of the most beautiful car in all the world. Just as me and Junior slept in our beds in the hotel, and poor Monte Slates in a bed in the guest room at Clutch's house, and Clutch stayed awake all night, watching that boy sleep, afraid the kid might try to run or the law or some vindictive fool might come after him, just as the night passed soundlessly and still and dark in the sky, a fire was lit and swallowed Junior's and mine and Clutch's brand-new car in flames.

It started right along the hood and crept back to the gas tank and blew the damn thing off its wheels and into the middle of the street. I heard the explosion and pulled myself out of my bed and met Junior in the hall and we ran on down the stairs and outside and somewhere in my heart and his we both knew it was too late, even before we could see the tumultuous waves of fire and flame, before we could hear the windows crack from the pressure and heat, before all the oil burned on out in a pool of black gunk and the headlights shattered and shot on out, before all that filled our lousy eyes, that single shot of an explosion from down on the street filled our ears and our hearts as a kind of resignation we already knew. Before we were down off the front porch and out on the lawn and the orange glow flickered across our sore lips, it was all already done in our heads and hearts.

"It's all over now." Junior frowned. "All over now."

"Mother of God," I mumbled, scratching my chin. "This just ain't right."

The fire swallowed that poor car whole, making it nothing more than a heavy black metal corpse. From where I stood on the curb, right beside Junior Breen, it seemed all his dreams, all his tiny hopes of some new kind of opportunity, had been set aflame and left to smolder dully in the middle of that black-paved street.

"It's done fer now," he sighed.

By the time one of La Harpie's three fire trucks arrived and me and Junior and even L.B., still low and unholy and still threatening Junior over his missing teeth, were all standing out on the curb across the street from where that fine automobile had been parked, we watched it smolder and burn.

"Serves you bastards right." L.B. smiled. His bald head shone with the fire. "Serves you two bastards right thinking you're such hot shit."

Everyone came out on their porch and watched the car burn. Everyone just stood there whispering to themselves in their night-clothes, muttering and nodding at me and Junior, casting all the aspersions they could carry over their thin gray lips and dirty white teeth.

"Look at the wheels melt." Junior frowned, sitting on the curb down the street from the hotel. The fire burned on as the firemen sprayed it down. "Look at that poor thing sag like that." He smiled a little, then lifted his head. "Hell, it still looks fast."

I patted his shoulder and spit at the ground. "This ain't right. You didn't have anything to do with Monte," I said. "I never should have let you come with me."

"I did it, not you. This is my own fault."

I watched the orange flames move through his eyes, fading along his face.

"Didn't think it would bring on anything like this. They all had to see that boy was being hurt."

Junior nodded. "This ain't over. You sure can feel it."

After that night, Junior Breen didn't say a damn word. He just locked himself in his room and sat there mumbling to himself until the next morning and didn't even bother showing up for work. That pretty ol' car had been his last hope. Nothing could remain close before it faded black and turned to dust. Not me or Clutch or little Monte Slates, not the car or the friends he made, not all the words he spelled out with his big hand or big hollow heart. Nothing could stay close before it became dull and empty of light.

Only her.

Only Eunice.

home

Come around the bend . . .

Down to the bank . . .

Come across the field and down to the bank . . .

Those days were like a crown of gold over her head. Her hair was a knotted nest of some tiny white and yellow flowers with little bluebells wrapped inside her curls. Maybe she'd bring him a sandwich or a bottle of Coca-Cola, all cold and full of beads of ice along the side. Wasn't it all so pretty? Wasn't it all so nice?

Then a thousand murmurs of the blade . . .

Then it was all gone and pushed far downstream.

Here was a man full of the grave old memories of his past. Junior would sit at work and stare out through the glass windows. He'd remember how it used to be, how it had been when he was still a boy, not more than fifteen, free and pure, without the most mortal of all sins holding him.

The best day in his life had been when he had saved Eunice from Forger Dunagree. He had seen something there in her eyes. He had seen something there of his own goodness hanging in the light above her head. She had promised him that he would become a smart man. A man with a nice clean soul.

"I'll show you my parts for less'n a quarter and let you kiss me in my ear if you want."

That Eunice was less than three years younger but smart as a whip and knew everything there was to know about making out and sex and having babies and French kissing. Eunice was the pretty little wild girl with deep red curls who would go around and kiss all the boys in school and offer them a full view of her private parts for a quarter or whatever pocket change they might have. There was nothing sinful or impure to it. Eunice was a girl who was proud of her own particularly high-spirited beauty and charm. That poor girl would shed her underpants at a moment's notice or go off and kiss you inside the mouth if you just dared her to. She was the kind of girl that had nearly married every boy in school by the sixth grade and there was nothing her mother or teachers or parson could do to stop her from growing up that way. This girl kept getting wilder and more and more beautiful each undelicate year she lived. There were boys all over town who had carved her name on their arms and promised to buy her a ten-thousand-acre pumpkin farm and a brand-new silver Cadillac if she'd run away with them when they were old enough to elope. This girl was a golden-stemmed flower among some worn swampland and weeds. This girl was something that was too sweet or pretty or pure to outlast the lifetime of a ten-cent kiss.

"Do you got a quarter or not?" she asked Forger Dunagree, blowing a hot breath in his ear. "Or are you chicken to see?"

"I ain't afraid to see." This Forger Dunagree was the dirtiest kid in Colterville. He was only about thirteen and was missing nearly all of his adult teeth. He lost most of them in fights with other dirty kids and the rest to tooth decay and gum disease. Forger's old man was a corn farmer who was known around town for getting drunk and falling asleep in his neighbors' yards, half undressed. Forger had run his old man down with the tractor once while the old drunkard was passed out in the field. He managed to lop off a good portion of his father's left foot before Forger heard his old man screaming. They had been too poor to afford plastic parts, so Mr. Dunagree replaced his lost appendage with cheap balsa wood that would sweat and creak when he walked.

"I ain't afraid to see naked parts. I got a stack of magazines like that at home in the back of my dresser drawer." Forger frowned. "Naked parts like that is old hat to me."

"That so?" Eunice smiled. "Bet you never got to give a pretty girl like me a kiss?"

"Whoever said you were pretty was just fooling you for kicks. You're about as pretty as a bug-eyed carp. Maybe a mealy-mouthed snail."

"Do you got a quarter or not?" Eunice sighed.

"I got four bucks. What'll I get for that?"

"'Cluding tax?" Eunice asked.

"Sure, sure, including tax."

"I pick your cherry for you right now." Eunice smiled.

"What?" Forger's face shot bright red. He felt sweat break out along his greasy little chin. "You make it for only four bucks?"

"Less than that. But it costs more 'cause you're so dirty." Eunice smiled.

"Fine." Forger smiled back. "Where you wanna go do it at?"

"Down by the riverbed. It's pretty quiet down there."

"All right." Forger smiled.

"Give me my money now." Eunice grinned.

"What for?"

"So I know you'll meet me there."

"What if you don't show?" Forger asked.

"Oh, I'll show, don't worry."

"But how do I know?"

"Here." Eunice sighed. She pressed her lips to his greasy

mouth and slipped her tongue inside. Forger's eyes snapped open huge and wide. He gave a little cough, then a smile.

"That's only part of it." Eunice grinned again. Forger nodded and dug into his pockets and handed her the four dollar bills. "Meet me down by the woodshed in about an hour."

"I sure will." Forger grinned and took off like a loose little dog. Eunice shook her head and kissed each one of the dollar bills.

"Boys are sure dumb."

Junior Breen had been trying to build a raft all summer long. Every time he'd find some scrap wood, it would be warped or full of holes or half-eaten with termites or just rotted through.

"Virtual infestation." He'd frown and throw the wood back on the muddy ground. He had gotten himself three good pieces. That was it. Barely enough to make a skiff. He had made himself a nice oar, shaved it on down from a two-by-four and nailed a paddle on the end. He wanted to build that raft and drift down the river to New Orleans and meet some voodoo priests and eat rice and red beans and run off with the French-speaking whores. He sat in that woodshed all summer long, trying to whittle himself out a dream from gnarled wood and the edge of a shortened hacksaw.

"Didn't think you'd show up." Forger smiled, wiping the sweat from his long narrow chin. "Thought you'd taken my money and made a fool of me."

"I wouldn't do that to you, Forger. Not to someone who lived so close to me."

They sat on the muddy bank, littered with dry brown leaves and rotten blackened wood and dirt and grassy green moss. The thin river wavered by, smelling hot and full of must. There was a whitish film along the edge and all kinds of yellowish insects skimming the surface in thick buzzing eaves. Eunice uncrossed her legs and took Forger's hand and planted it on her own chest.

"Close your eyes," she whispered. Forger nodded and did. He

smiled and licked his lips. Eunice reached down and unbuckled his dirty gray corduroys at the snap. Forger made a little mumble.

"Now keep your eyes closed," Eunice said. He nodded. She reached down and touched him just below the waist. Then she pulled his pants down around his knees. He had a pair of old gray-and-white tight skivvies on. They were worn and threadbare and tight around his groin.

"Now don't move," she whispered. He nodded again. She put her hand over Forger's eyes and placed his hand against her chest. He could feel the beat down there, *thump-thump, thump-thump,* soft and clean and potent as spring. He felt the back of his legs aching as she breathed against his ear. Eunice laid her body right beside his, still covering his eyes, still breathing in his ear. She slipped his skivvies down and gave a little giggle.

"That's it?" she snickered, shaking her head.

Forger shot up and pulled up his pants. His face flashed bright red. "What? What's wrong?"

"It's too small. I've got myself a bigger pinky finger than that." She gave a little frown. "Let's just forget the whole thing."

"But my four dollars . . ."

"But nothing. You're lucky I don't go around and tell everyone in school."

"I want my money back."

"You want your money back?" Eunice smiled. "Here you go." She dug into the front of her dress and held out the soft green folds of cash. "Everyone in town's gonna know what a little pecker you have. Everyone's gonna laugh and shout and make jokes about it. Even your whiskey-drinking old man. He might take you out in the barn and try to stretch it out for you."

The trick always worked. Every boy that had paid Eunice a red cent had lost their money on account of their small privates and unfounded fear.

"That's fine." She smiled. Eunice closed her hand and folded up the cash and put it back in her dress.

"You got an awful big mouth. Jim Ginerly said you told him the same thing and backed on out with him, too."

"It's not my fault you boys all have small parts." She tried to smile. Forger gripped her hard around her wrist and pushed her down on her back, then climbed on top.

"I don't think I care." Forger smiled. "You're going to do it anyway."

He began to push up the folds of her white dress when a thick gray shadow fell hard over him. It cut straight through the heat and the dampness and the steady muddy ground, making everything cold and solemn and still.

"Take your hands on off." Junior frowned, holding the hacksaw tight in his hand. "Take your hands on off 'fore I separate them from your wrists."

Forger nodded and hopped off.

"Junior, we were just wrestling is all . . ."

"Go on. Get 'fore I split you in two."

"But she took my money, Junior. She took it from me unfair."

"You wanna walk with a limp?" Junior asked, placing the blade against Forger Dunagree's knee.

"You make it with her, too, huh? She takes you out back here and gives it to you?"

Junior slammed his big wide forearm up against Forger's chin, knocking him clear off his feet. Forger landed on his back in the mud, gritting his teeth.

"Now get," Junior grunted, holding the hacksaw tight.

"You are a little whore!" Forger shouted, wobbling to his feet. "You're a whore and everyone knows!!" He stumbled away, spitting the blood from out of his teeth.

Eunice stood and straightened out her dress, then shook her head.

"My hero." She frowned. "When are you gonna let me take care of myself?"

"Doesn't look like you were doing such a good job."

"Maybe not to you. But I took Forger back here 'cause I knew you'd be working in there. I knew I wasn't in any trouble at all." Eunice gave a little smile. "Did you hear us making it?" She gave a little sigh, then a wink. "It was so wicked. I can still feel all the sin burning along my skin."

"Hush, Eunice, why do you have to talk like that?"

"It's what makes the boys pay, isn't it?" Eunice dug into her dress and handed him the four dollars. "Here, you earned it more than me."

Junior shook his head.

"You keep it and buy yourself some manners. Maybe you won't have to go lying in the mud for friends then."

Eunice gave a little huff, then stuck her money back in her dress and crossed her arms in front of her chest.

"How's the raft coming today?" she asked.

"Slow as syrup." He frowned. "Slow as your own dubious grace."

"Hush, Junior, why do you gotta talk like that?" Eunice let out a little laugh, then stood on her tiptoes and kissed Junior's cheek. "A smart fellow like you could make some girl's heart ache. You know, you're gonna grow up to be the most handsome, smartest fellow in town. And everyone will call you Mr. Junior and all the ladies will fight over every one of your words. Every one, I bet. You'll be the nicest man anywhere around."

"Thanks." Junior smiled, shaking his head. "How much you charge the boys for a good prevarication like that?"

"What?"

"A nice lie like that? How much do you usually charge?"

"That one's free. Hey, I know what I oughta do. I should go spend that money on a dictionary so someone can half-understand what it is you're saying when you speak. Maybe I'll just go get myself a malted and some steak fries instead." Eunice shrugged her shoulders and gave a little smile. "See you later, Mr. Junior Breen."

Junior smiled and watched her creep out through the woods down the bank. Later that day, he found the nice red dictionary, bound tight in red leather, sitting out all alone out by the woodshed door. There was no note or letter saying who it was from. But he knew. He always knew. Eunice had surely stolen it from the elementary school.

He would always love her.

He would always love her poor unholy soul.

Junior felt his body tighten under the sweaty white sheets.

It was all a cruel kind of dream. Nothing beside him but his lonely bed and the night.

But she was still there. In the room. Right behind the closet door. Breathing there still. He shot out of bed and pulled on the closet hard. It was locked. Nailed shut. He dug under his mattress for the cold gray hammer and pried its silvery claw between the frame and the door, digging at a long metal nail, forcing it with all his strength and weight. He jammed the edge of the claw-hammer under the next nail's head and slid it on out, then the next, then the next, until there was a shiny silver halo of spikes left cold and dull along the floor. He left the last two in and gripped the doorknob and pulled, tearing the wood from its frame. The wood creaked and struggled but finally gave. Then it was quiet. Then there was nothing but the voice he so badly wanted to hear.

Eunice . . .

He stepped on inside.

Eunice . . .

Nothing there. There was nothing in there but the dark and the dust of the past.

But he had heard her breath. He had heard her voice in his dreams.

Eunice . . .

Nothing had been there all along.

He fell to his knees, beginning to sob, leaning his face against the dull wood frame, still seeing her lying there in the light, all alone and undone, broken in pieces by the thin hacksaw he had used.

Go around the bend . . .

Sink on down . . .

Disappear . . .

Don't come back around.

There's nothing here whispering.

There's nothing here for me to hear or feel.

There's nothing here but the cold red tributaries of my own sin.

old red organ

Doing it in a motel bed and breaking parole seemed like a fine idea at first. I wanted to get out of that town as soon as I could. I wanted to have intimacies with my Charlene like a normal man and his girl should. I had stolen some cash from where I worked and ran a baby down trying to escape, but now I was something worse. I had helped burn up Mr. Slates's face when I was nothing more than a convict myself. Also, I had stolen Earl Peet's girl. Everywhere I went in town, people would whisper and stare at me. That poor little baby in the blue carriage had already been laid in the ground. But that damn fool Earl Peet was still walking around.

"Do you wanna take a drive with me up to Baliboo? My Aunt Fiona finally died and my cousin Twilla needs some help with the arrangements." Charlene was holding my hand and leaning against me.

"Why sure." I smiled. "Stay a couple of nights in a fancy motel bed? Make love on a mattress instead of a parking brake?"

"Oh, wait a minute. I forgot. It's over the state line. I won't have you breaking parole on account of me."

"So what? If we go for the weekend, we'll make it back before anyone ever knows."

So we went.

I took three days of vacation time and we made it away. Charlene drove the whole three hours up to Baliboo, Wisconsin, with me singing and making jokes and grabbing her thighs, and somewhere just over that state line a precious little thought occurred to me and reminded me of something Guy Gladly had told me. The world does not end with that tiny scrub of a town. Sitting in the passenger seat of that car, watching Charlene, seeing the whole bright world flash by, I got the feeling that she and I were not only driving, but moving straight ahead. We were moving past it all, moving right by, with her beautiful brown hair blowing like a halo around her head and her sweet delicate voice whispering in my ear. It made me want to drive all night. It made me want to stay in that car with her and drive and drive until all the things I had ever lost or known were long gone. Charlene's foot was heavy, and we made it to her crazy aunt's place in three hours.

It was an old gray, gloomy house, withered and soaked in despair. It made Charlene squeeze my hand as soon as she caught sight of it. It broke any good mood right away. Nothing about it seemed alive save for the small black birds that were perched still and sullen, singing little whistling hymns in the low trees.

"There it is." Charlene smiled. "Me and Ullele used to sit in those swings out front for hours and talk about boys. She told me once if you wanted a boy to love you, you had to kiss his lips, then say a quick prayer to the Virgin Mary, and then say his name a hundred times every night before you went to sleep."

"Does it work?" I asked.

"How do you think I got you?"

Those nice chain swings swung from a fat maple tree out front, dangling just above the overrun grass and weeds. The house itself was a real sad sight all right, getting worse as we stepped close. A whole section of the porch had begun to sink and lean in on itself. There was a broken window or two on the second floor and crabweed and black vines growing up the side. There were all kinds of holes dug into the wood paneling along the top floor, and nests and hunks of weeds growing right along the gutters and the roof. It looked sad. I watched Charlene take it all in and shake her head.

"It didn't used to be like this. There was a nice garden out on the side there and wind chimes on the porch. It used to be the prettiest house ever. I used to pretend that I'd get married to some professional race car driver and we'd move in here and I'd sit out on the porch every night waiting for my husband to come home from the races and then he'd come from over the hill there and carry me up the stairs to that big silver four-poster bed and we'd sit up there and kiss and watch the sunset and stay awake as long as we liked." Charlene gave a little sigh and tried to smile. "It seems all the things I ever wanted are pretty far away."

I squeezed her hand and helped her up the porch as the whole house gave a little creak.

"My daddy would have a heart attack if he saw the place like this." She frowned.

"Why didn't your folks come?" I asked.

"There was some pretty bad blood between my daddy and his sister. She wouldn't be beholden to anyone. She was that kind of woman. When my father offered to pay for her to be put in a rest home, she told him to take all his money and go to hell. My daddy, well, you know how he is, he kept a grudge against her after that and they stopped talking altogether. When my cousin called to tell us the news, my daddy just shook his head and said she'd already been dead to him for years already."

I nodded and kissed her cheek. "It's nice of you to come up here like this. I'll bet your aunt would appreciate it kindly."

"I wanted to see the house again and her and just try to make it all nice in my mind."

Charlene knocked on the door and her crazy cousin Twilla swung it open with a scream. "Charlene!!!" she howled. "You came!! You really made it! You came!!"

Twilla was something of a lunatic, I guess. She had been raised on a dog farm, and one night when she was sixteen she went out and shot all the puppies dead with her daddy's Winchester because the boy she loved didn't ask her to the Spring Dance. I had a feeling most of the women in Charlene's family suffered some sort of mental problem, though, not through any fault of their own. It seemed to me these crazy ladies were mostly lonely, lonely by themselves or with their own families around, and no one cared or noticed until some blood had been shed or something turned up dead in the yard. It seemed all these ladies suffered from each having a lonely kind of heart.

"This is Luce." Charlene smiled, introducing me.

Twilla kissed my cheek and shook my hand. "Nice to meet you, Luce. Nice of you to drive all the way up here with Charlene."

"Nice to meet you, too," I said.

"So has everything been arranged?" Charlene asked. "Did you need some help with anything?"

"Nope, it's all taken care of. Aunt Fiona's upstairs."

"Upstairs?" Charlene asked.

"Yes. Lord, that's the way she wanted it. Wrote it down in her will. She wanted to be kept up in her room for at least seven days so all her kids could be sure she wasn't just up there asleep. She started losing her mind there at the end. The house started falling apart and there was no one around to help her keep it up, with me at the hospital and, well, you and your sisters all over the place. So she got lonely up here, I guess. Started letting little animals inside the house. Let them damn squirrels ruin the place. It was a kindly thing to do, I guess, open up her house, but creepy just the same."

"That was her way." Charlene frowned. "Is she all right to see?"

"I guess. But you might not want to go up there. You haven't seen her in some time and it might be a kind of shock."

"It's OK." Charlene smiled. "I'd like to say goodbye if I have the chance." She squeezed my hand and then started to walk up the stairs. I began to follow and then Charlene stopped and stared at me with a frown. "Luce, you don't have to come along," she whispered.

"It's OK," I mumbled. "You can prop me up in case I faint."

Charlene gave a warm little smile and took my hand and we walked the three flights of stairs to the top floor without another word. I felt myself beginning to sweat. I was getting nervous as hell. Charlene turned the rusty gold doorknob at the top of the landing and opened the door a little bit.

Mothballs seemed to tumble on out. That musty dusty scent began to cloud my eyes as I followed Charlene and stepped inside, staring at all the holes dug into the walls and through the floor to the light outside. Cool blue light covered everything, streaming across the floor, making shadows every step we took from all kinds of holes in the floorboards and walls. There was the silver four-poster bed, bright and wooden and draped with a dark purple veil. There was the old lady's shape, resting in place, covered with a dark blanket up to her white little chin. Her long gray hair rose above her head and over her shoulders and nearly reached the floor. It appeared she hadn't cut her hair in a few hundred years.

In that room, something else was breathing. Making a desperate little plea.

We stepped closer, holding hands, and we were about two feet from the bed when I noticed something moving right above that old lady's face.

A bird.

There was a tiny goddamn sparrow nested in the huge gray tangle of her hair. Then I looked again and saw another bird propped up beside her ear. That old lady laid in her bed with a nest of birds in her goddamn hair. I stopped where I was. Then something skittered across the floor and I tried not to shout. Charlene gave a little start. This little thing skittered back and forth and then under the bed. A squirrel. A goddamn squirrel. There were all kinds of animals living in the goddamn hair on her head and in the room where she was lying in her most final of reprieves.

Charlene squeezed my hand and took one step closer, then turned away. "She looks like an angel lying there," she whispered.

I nodded and watched as a bird appeared from behind a pillow and then took flight and crept outside through one of the holes in the side wall. It was too much of a sight. There was another tiny sparrow resting on the old lady's lips. It looked like the damn thing was giving her the softest, most delicate kiss it could deliver. It nested right there on her lips and gave a little chirp as a kind of sweet reply to all the things that old dead lady might be whispering. I could hear the sounds of that bird breathing. The sound inside its throat. It was humming. It was humming and staring right at me. I tried to close my eyes, to block it all out, but I could still hear its little heart beating in its throat and its little beak breaking open and closed, I could hear its tiny sharp fingers holding tight to that old lady's skin, stealing her soul as she slept in that dark purple bed. I left Charlene there to have a moment or two alone, deciding it might be best if I waited down the stairs.

After a while, I went outside and found Charlene sitting in her swing out front, humming a little song out there all alone to herself.

It had already begun to get dark. The sun had just begun to set and night was rolling in like a single cloud from the west.

Charlene sat in her nice old silver swing, barely moving at all, hanging there, suspended in place. She could have waited there long as she liked and she'd still be the most beautiful sight I'd ever see.

"How do." I smiled, bent over, kissing her cheek. She placed her head warmly against my chest and I took a seat in the other swing, dragging my feet underneath me in the little bit of dirt and grass. "How you doing there, pal?" I asked, staring at the way her head was hung kind of low, like it was all weighed down pretty heavy with some unwieldy thoughts.

Charlene gave a little smile and twitched her nose.

"In heaven, there are cradles of gold," she murmured in one soft breath. "That's what my crazy aunt used to tell me. Told me there's a whole long place filled with golden cribs full of baby angels waiting to be born. That's what she used to tell me where babies came from."

"That sounds sweet." I smiled.

Charlene nodded and looked down at her bare feet. Then she said something quick, with a soft little smile and twinkle in her eye and a pass of her hand right through her tousled brown hair, and after she said it, I thought I might just about die.

"I think I'm preggers, Luce Lemay."

My heart skipped a full breathing beat.

It hit me like a sucker punch right in my teeth. I fell right out of that tiny silver chain swing and on my behind and looked up at her, feeling my heart shaking somewhere down around my waist.

"Come again?" I sputtered, cotton-mouthed as all hell. I couldn't breathe. I couldn't make a sound. All the words in the world had become frozen and unfamiliar to me just as she lowered her hair and said it again.

"I'm in the family way, Luce. I'm late by four days. I've never been this late before in my life. I feel it, too, I think. I've been trying to think of some way to tell you the last few days. But I just couldn't let it wait. Sitting here thinking about it, I thought I shouldn't let it wait."

I nodded. In that moment, everything changed.

"A baby . . ." I mumbled.

"That's right, fella. A baby. And I'm too old to be praying some angel might miss its turn and skip over me." She placed her hand against her cheek and closed her lips. "This is it. I'm pretty sure I can feel it."

I got right up out of the mud and kissed her lips. They were not so tender and soft. They were tight. They were tight and trembling and scared as rabbits. I put her hand in mine and she laid her face against my chest.

"I'm scared, Luce. I'm twenty-five. What if this is the only chance I get? I don't wanna miss it. I don't wanna give it away or get married or get myself fixed or do whatever you're supposed to do when something happens like this. I wanna keep it. I've thought about it and even if you split town, I want to keep it because it's part of me and full of nothing but love."

By now Charlene was crying and muffling it in my shirt and I was all broken up and teary-eyed and still fighting to think of something to say.

"You don't think we should get married?" I muttered.

"No," she whispered. "No, it's not right. We're sure not ready to get married, and bringing up a baby is hard enough without trying to figure you and me and us all out." She looked away. "I'm just not ready for any of this . . ." she sobbed, clinging tight to my shirt.

"Guess I just don't know," I said. "Guess I don't know what we're supposed to do."

Charlene just shook her head and cried some more.

"I guess you've just gotta take what's good around you and love it right now," I mumbled. "That's how I feel anyway. I'm not saying we should get married or anything you don't wanna do, but it seems to me this is a kind of gift and we'd be damn fools to screw it up just because it's something scary and new. But you know how I feel about you. You know I wouldn't do anything to hurt you. And seeing you like this makes me wish I had never laid a hand on you. But then there's a part of me that's scared and happy and glad as hell. There's a part of me that's sure if I could take it back somehow, I know I wouldn't. This is something special between the two of us and I'll do whatever you want me to do but leave you, because you're the most important person in the world to me and this is a blessing and we should take whatever good things we're able to."

"Guess that's one way of looking at it." She smiled, then she leaned back and pulled all her hair back into a ponytail and tied it up tight, knotting it there like a kind of promise, a kind of quiet agreement to what I had just said. Then we both just sat there quiet and still.

"Do you wanna get hitched? Or is it just getting hitched to me that seems so bad?" I asked.

"No, it's not that. I'm just scared, Luce. I'm scared for you and me and what my parents are going to say and what we're gonna do when this baby's born."

"But it's a good kind of scared. It's being scared but full of hope. Hope of all the good things that might come," I said.

Charlene leaned in close to me and I kissed her neck. Then we sat there without saying a word for a few minutes more.

"Hitched, huh?" she said, rolling her brown eyes.

"It might not be so bad. There's worse reasons to get married than this."

"Like what?" she asked.

"Well, like money for instance. Or because you don't think you can find anyone else. I think we got something here. We got something here we don't have to put into words, Charlene."

"It might be nice." She smiled.

"Well, heck, I don't hear you going on and on about how you feel. The only way I'm sure of how you feel is when we're kissing or doing things like that. Most of the other times you're a kind of mystery to me."

"Hmph." She frowned, shaking her head.

"It just seems right to me. I mean, we could save up some money and maybe move out West or put a down payment on a mobile home. But this is the start of something, Charlene. This is the start of something great. I think you might feel it, too." I took a deep breath and stared at her face. "What do you say?"

This pretty lady leaned over and kissed my lips in a soft breath. "I do, Luce Lemay." She leaned in so close, so gentle beside me. Her skin seemed so smooth and bright that I wanted to kiss her and keep kissing her until the night had fallen all around us like a delicate screen and we could be alone in the field together for a long, long time, not worried about ever going back to La Harpie.

That night we made it in the Blue Moon Motel a few miles down the road, in a bed, between nice white sheets, like a real couple, like a man and a woman should, holding each other tight, sleeping in each other's arms all night until the sweet-faced Mexican maid came to our door in the morning and told us we had an hour before checkout, and that was fine because it was all just a little glimpse, a single little glimmer of what it would all be like someday not too far away.

We headed on back the next night, after all the arrangements for Aunt Fiona had been made, with Charlene beaming and me holding her hand as she kept one hand on the steering wheel, not driving back, but straight ahead and away from the past. Everything was perfect there in the night. Everything was perfect and sweet and good with the two of us all alone out on the road, sharing one beautiful dream.

Just before we got back to La Harpie, I had a terrible thought. I thought it and made the mistake of saying it before I could catch myself.

"Maybe we should wait."

"Huh?" Charlene whispered, half-dreaming.

"Maybe we should be sure before we go and tell anybody about the baby, I mean."

"Oh," she said. "If you like."

"I just . . . I mean, I hope you'd still want to consider marrying me, but if, well, that changes how you feel, I'd understand."

"You don't sound so sure yourself."

"No, I just don't want you to, *us*, I mean, to jump into anything. We might as well be sure."

"I guess," she said looking away. "I'm sure, even if there isn't a baby."

I looked down at her hands on the wheel. "I've just gotten through one too many mistakes already. I wouldn't want, well, you to be another one, too."

"Maybe it is a mistake then."

"Charlene . . . I was just thinking of how you might feel differently."

"Maybe you were thinking of how *you* might feel," she said.

"Charlene . . ."

"Don't," she said. "Just let it go. Let it go."

She pulled up in front of the dingy red-brick St. Francis Hotel and closed her eyes. Then I felt my lips trembling and wanted to say it all, tell her everything I ever felt, but it all seemed so wrong and selfish and small that I just turned and kissed her lips and hoped and prayed I'd be able to kiss her again at the end of some other day not too far away.

"Please come by and see me at work tomorrow," I said. "I don't wanna screw up the only good thing I have. We'll work this out. I know we can. I think we can, at least."

"It's just . . ." she muttered, trying to keep in her tears. But they trickled on out and crossed down her face and she turned away, crying into the steering wheel.

"I know," I mumbled. "Anything is hard that's worth anything you'd like to keep."

I kissed her once more, again, not for me or her but for the future a tender touch like that might hopefully bring.

"Good night," she murmured. "I'm sorry for getting pregnant and tying you down here now. You're the best thing I've ever had close to me and I've let you and myself down, too."

"Charlene . . ."

She sat on up and wiped her eyes, then stared straight ahead. "If there is a heaven, there's no gold cradles up there, I swear."

Then she pulled away and I felt like everything we had dreamt about had suddenly gone dark and faded to gray.

Time takes care of all things, true or not.

There was no baby after all. Charlene got her period a day later and called me up at work with the news and when I asked her if she was relieved she just gave a little sigh and said, "Guess so, I guess." But it was a thing she didn't have to say out loud. A little tiny dream between us had ceased to be real, and for all the talking and kissing and hoping and worrying and being afraid, there was nothing to say that would make it all seem like everything was still the same. It had been a fine idea but now it seemed kind of useless and far away. I didn't mention a thing about my lowly kind of proposal and she didn't say anything about the two of us running on away, so we just left it all at that and when the phone was hung up on the wall and the receiver put back in its place, I couldn't help but kind of wish it had all gone the other way and the two of us were about to get hitched and have a kid and a house or a mobile home and be spending the rest of our time together, instead of me standing there in that gas station wishing for it like that, all alone, staring at the hollow blue phone.

No, it didn't seem fair, it didn't seem fair or just or good at all. I felt like the two of us had gotten pretty close and now she might be feeling like me, kind of lonely, kind of confused and scared, and when I called her back to try to talk about it all, someone else at the diner answered the phone and said Charlene was tied up. Then it occurred to me. Then I was sure that the death of a little dream is about the worst thing anyone can feel when you're already kind of low and in need of any good idea or thing with some blessed hope of its own. It's not something easy to explain. It's not something I could put right into words. But I was sure. Made sure by the way I had felt holding Charlene in that motel bed for that one single lovely night, made dumb now by the dark empty space it left once that nice little illusion had been put gently to rest.

It stung me right in the hollow of my sweaty white palm.

It stung me as I knocked that poor blue phone off the goddamn wall and clear out of my goddamn sight once and for all.

christ told the woman at the well

A burning secret is made into something much worse once it's told.

"It is only a matter of time before it muddies us all," Junior muttered, scratching with the stick.

Junior and I walked on home from the Gas-N-Go, toting a six-pack of beer between us. He had met me at work because he was feeling lonesome. I was feeling as lonesome as hell, too. I was waiting for someone to shoot me in the back of the head. The thing between me and Charlene had been made uncomfortable and strange, a kind of false little play, and neither of us knew what to do now or what to say to make it all the way it had been before, so it was beginning to fade away, fade into something scared and still and cold. I hadn't talked to her in about a week. All the time I was at work, I thought about her. But it didn't do any good. I wanted to call her, I held the phone in my hand and dialed it a thousand times, but all the words I thought to say disappeared as soon as it rang.

I put the cold can of Pabst Blue Ribbon to my lips and tried to drown it all. Junior mumbled something to himself and I stared at him with a frown.

Poor Junior was feeling pretty low on his own. He was already pretty drunk when he arrived at the Gas-N-Go. He had been mumbling something to himself all night. Now that crazy fool was composing a poem in the dirt along the side of the road as we stumbled along.

"Tonight I can seeeee," he murmured, and scratched into the dirt with the end of a long narrow stick. "Pearls and plums of heaven and splendor solid as your precious white teeth. Left in the dust. In the d-u-s-t."

"Now what the hell does that mean?" I asked, taking a long slug from my silver beer can. "To who the hell is this one addressed, may I ask?"

"Here are the ends of your tiny toes all along the edge of this narrow, narrow road," he mumbled, and scratched some of that in the dirt, too. "All the things we could have loved have turned to mud. Mud, mud, mud." He stopped, finished off his beer, and crushed the can in his hand.

"That's not such a romantic sentiment." I frowned. "Not at all."

Junior shrugged his shoulders and scratched the stick into the dirt some more, mumbling the rest to himself. I could hear him breathing. There was no other sound around. We walked on. Some yellow headlights appeared behind us, moving steadily, shining golden and bright. Junior and I stepped aside, down into the dirt of the shoulder of the road, as the yellow headlights flashed right upon us, then stopped. It was a dark black Chevy. It idled right there, kicking up some dust, until the doors flew open and a kind of fire poured on out.

I knew it. I knew just what was about to unfold upon our lowly skulls. Four or five bastards with masks tied around their faces ran right for us, carrying planks of wood and baseball bats.

"Christ," I heard myself mumble. One of the men in a red mask hit Junior in the shoulder with the side of a thick wooden baseball bat. Louisville Slugger. The name echoed in my teeth.

Junior grunted, then swung and smacked the man somewhere beneath his red mask, knocking the bastard off his feet. Another one of the men clipped Junior in the back of the head with the end of a wood plank. Junior staggered forward, then held the spot where he had been hit. Some thick red blood flooded out through his fingers and down along his back.

"No!!" I shouted, and lunged for one of them, digging my fingers into a soft white throat. Someone cracked me in the eye with the side of a board. I turned to take a swing at him, but someone else knocked me in the back of the head with a bat and sent me down into the dirt. He hit me again in the head and I felt my ear ring with pain as I slumped to the ground on my back. Junior grunted something, then cracked one of them in the face with the six-pack. Some blood flickered through the night. Junior dropped the cans and grabbed one of the men around his throat. He squeezed hard until some other man hit him in the side of his head with a wooden board. Junior let out a howl and turned, knocking the board out of the man's hand, just as some other bastard jumped up on his back and wrapped his thick forearm around Junior's portly throat. The other four men began hitting Junior in his wide chest with their boards and baseball bats, until Junior began coughing up blood and fell to his knees, then his face, twitching and spitting up bits of crimson in the dirt.

"We got the story on you both. Heard you cut up a poor little girl in Colterville."

Someone swung a baseball bat against Junior's tiny little ear. Just then, Sheriff Fontane spun down the road in his squad car, lights flashing. The five men got back in the black Chevy and pulled away quick. Sheriff Fontane hurried beside us and began praying quietly.

I couldn't move. Junior rolled on his side, holding his bleeding ear, then pulled himself beside me.

"Luce . . ." he whispered. "You OK?"

I couldn't make the words come out right.

"We need to get him out of the road," the sheriff whispered, holding my hand.

Junior pulled himself to his feet, wobbling at the knees. He coughed up some vomit and blood, then pulled himself up straight again. He kept coughing and wheezing as he bent over and grabbed me under my arm, pulling me to my feet. I couldn't stand. My goddamn knees were too weak. All the blood in my head felt like it was leaking out one end.

"Sweet Jesus, Luce," Junior mumbled through some blood. "Your goddamn eyeball is half outta your head."

He grabbed me tight under my arm and held me close and dragged me into the sheriff's car. We made it to the St. Francis Hotel.

"I'll go fetch a doctor," the sheriff said. "The best thing you can do now is take the next bus out of town. I'm saddened to say it, but you two ought to leave as soon as you can," he added, then sped away.

Junior pulled me up the stairs and down the hall. I could feel him dragging me over the soft red carpet, pulling me along my back toward my room at the end of the hall.

The door across the hall from mine opened wide as Junior fumbled through my pockets for my keys.

"Hell!!" L.B. shouted. "What the hell happened to you boys?"

Junior let some blood roll over his teeth as he unlocked my door and dragged me inside. L.B. followed, looking down at me, whistling as Junior wrapped a dirty T-shirt around my swollen eye.

"That boy is a mess," L.B. whispered. "Looks like you caught some of it, too." He smiled to Junior, running his pink tongue over his empty upper gums.

I opened my eye just once and saw L.B.'s empty pink gums,

then covered my face with the rest of the T-shirt. I woke up when the doctor arrived. This doctor had a big silver head of hair and small foxlike eyes and a black medicine bag, and he whistled at me when Junior uncovered the bloody shirt from my eye.

"Sweet lord," the doctor mumbled. "What happened to this man?"

"Ran into his past." L.B. frowned, scratching his chin. He gave a little grunt, nodding to himself. The doctor cleaned out the wound around my eye and put a white cloth patch over the socket and some salve along the side of my face and did the same for Junior, who sat by my bed the whole time. Old Lady St. Francis came in and muttered some prayers and shook her head and kissed my hand, then Junior made her leave and I rolled over on my side and tried to keep my eyes shut tight.

I fell asleep for a while but woke up in the middle of the night, my head throbbing and humming dully with a low kind of pain. It kept humming in my head and ears. Then I realized it wasn't the pain. I was mumbling last names. I was trying to figure out all the men who had been there. I was sure one of them had been Earl Peet.

The thing I couldn't figure out was how they found out about Junior like that. I mean, myself, I had been born in that town. But Junior, no one knew about his past. Someone had told them. Someone had let them know.

Then it hit me. It hit me right straight in my eye as I was finally falling back asleep.

The board across my teeth. The sound of Junior busting someone's cheek.

"We got the story on you both. Heard you cut up a poor little girl in Colterville."

Those missing teeth. Those grinning gums.

L.B.

He had told them everything. No one else but me and L.B. knew that much about Junior Breen. Junior had known L.B. to be another con and had trusted him with the truth of why he had been sent to the pen, and that L.B. had let it all out.

I pulled myself out of bed in the middle of the night and staggered across the hall. I knocked once, then fell against the door.

"Christ, Luce, whatcha doing out of bed?" L.B. mumbled. He pulled me to my feet and helped me back across the hall and into my own bed. "Now stay put, you dumb bastard."

"It was you, wasn't it?" I mumbled. "It was you."

"What?"

"It was you who told them about Junior, wasn't it?" I asked.

"Didn't tell anyone a thing but the truth."

I gritted my teeth.

"They were supposed to only rough you boys up a little."

"You don't know what you just did," I mumbled. "You don't know what you did."

"That big fool started this whole thing. He took my goddamn teeth. My goddamn teeth!! Hell, I didn't know those boys were gonna do this to you. You gotta know that's the honest to God truth."

"Those are kind words," I muttered, spitting as I spoke. "Awful kind words."

L.B. slammed my door closed and I climbed back into my bed. I buried my face in the sheets and tried to fall asleep, shaking and shivering through dark silent dreams.

buried treasure

I lay on my back in my bed, trying not to ever open those awful peepholes again.

The whole lousy thing that had happened made me miss my poor mom and dad. Wish I had some blood of my own to care for me. Someone I loved to watch over me. I wouldn't let Junior get a hold of Charlene. I didn't want her to see me all busted up and her to think it was somehow her fault. But then I was alone the whole day after our beating took place. Junior was at work and both my folks were far and gone and I was all alone feeling like I didn't have anyone to fall back on.

I took the bus on out to my old house. My left eye was bandaged up and the other was bruised and gray. People kept staring at me as they climbed on the bus, so I got off a few stops early and walked the rest of the way.

My house looked nice and white now. Someone sweet had moved in, you could tell. There were flowers planted out front and a few bicycles left in the yard and a nice front porch swing hanging in place along the white wood porch. It looked nice. It looked like it meant something to somebody.

I blinked my right eye and gave a little cough. I leaned against

the nice fence and covered my mouth. Both my eyes were still sore
as hell. They still felt ready to pop on out. I stared over the fence
with my right eye and into my old backyard. It hadn't changed
much in all these years. The people living there still kept hogs, but
now there was a soft-bellied cow and a few chickens scurrying
around scratching in the dirt.

I looked down at my own hands. I looked down at the dull
and fading tattoos that were inked along my wrists. The sacred
heart burned there, fiery and still. I had gotten that when I was
sixteen. On my other arm was an Oriental dragon. My friend, a
con, Nathan Beavers, had done that one with a tattoo gun he had
made from a Walkman radio while we were in jail. That dragon
was black and poorly done but it still meant something to me. Its
jaws were open, baring its teeth, and fire was racing all around its
wings. He had done it for me for five bucks and a pack of cigarettes. He had done it because we were both locked away and
needed a sign that we were still both free. I thought about those
tattoos. I wondered now if they made me doomed, if they showed
what kind of lowly desperate man I really was. I thought about
Clutch's tattoo. He had a nice voluptuous hula girl in a green grass
skirt right on his forearm. It made him seem kind of free. It made
him seem closer to something that wasn't tied down or ignorant or
full of fear. It made him seem closer to the truth all right, and
some kind of well-deserved pride.

I stared at that old white house for a long time, leaning against
the rickety white wood fence, until a towheaded kid came outside.
He had a dirty face and was missing a few teeth and was laughing
to himself and started rolling right in the dirt.

"Hey, kid, there's a big glass jar of pennies buried right under
that porch. If you can find 'em under there, they're all yours," I
said. I had saved all the pennies I could find for three summers
and buried them under the porch in case I ever found myself in an

emergency. I had never dug them up. They were still sitting under there, waiting to be set free. It seemed good as any other time. It seemed time to me.

This kid pulled himself to his small awkward feet and scratched his face for a while. "A jar of pennies? Is that true, mister?"

"Sure is."

"Thanks!"

His tiny blue eyes lit up like magic as he crawled under the porch and began digging, singing some made-up song to himself. He plowed right through the soft dry dirt with a long narrow stick, moving his head from side to side as he whistled and hummed and smiled. I stood there a moment longer, until I could very nearly hear my own mother calling me on inside. I needed to do what was right. I needed to be a man. Do the thing that was hard and make a stand. It didn't make all that much sense to me. But it wasn't a choice I had to make alone. There was Junior and the sheriff and Charlene and Clutch, they'd all stand by me to judge a man on his past. A past he served, a debt he paid. Maybe it isn't all as simple as time in jail. It hadn't been for me. Maybe it's a debt you can't ever repay. When it came down to it, it wasn't about the things we had done, it wasn't about the crimes we had laid with our own hands, it wasn't even about us, it came down to what kind of men believed they had the right to lay judgment.

I spat hard in the dirt and began the walk back to the hotel. The sun had gone completely from the sky. This was not a matter of pride. It was a matter of hope. The hope to be redeemed.

There was nothing else this town could do to me now.

last words at the bus depot

I walked into the Starlite to tell Charlene what I had decided. We still weren't reconciled. I refused to see her. I couldn't stare into her sweet face and have her staring back at me with a busted-up eye and bruises up and down my chin. So she kept calling me at work, crying, telling me how it was all her fault, me getting hurt, but the both of us knew it just wasn't true. I had gotten myself into this predicament and there was no one else to blame but me.

So there was the waitress of all my hope, Charlene, serving a nice piece of blueberry pie to a bald man with silvery white teeth. She set the plate down and smiled, then turned and caught sight of me and gave a little start.

"Luce . . ." she whispered. "Oh my God, Luce . . ."

Her sweet brown eyes began to swell up with tears right away and she started to run into the back to cry, but I caught hold of her hand and walked with her to the shiny silver counter, mumbling her name the whole time.

"Oh, Luce, what did they do to you?"

Charlene looked up at the white bandage that ran over the left side of my face. I tried to give a little smile to let her know I was OK, but I wasn't, and all I could offer was a wee little grin that showed all the deep-blue-and-black bruises gathered right under my chin.

"My god . . . I'm so sorry, Luce . . . I'm so sorry . . ."

She began to cry again, so I squeezed her hand tight and tried turning my face away a little so she wouldn't have to stare at all that unpleasantness straight on.

"I came here to tell you something, Charlene, not to make you cry."

"Tell me something? Jesus, Luce, how can you even talk to me?"

"This isn't your fault and you and I know it."

Charlene shook her head, still crying. "Are you leaving on the bus tonight?"

I gritted my teeth together and shook my head. "That's what I came to tell you." I took a deep breath and let it all out. "I'm staying," I said in a short mumbled breath.

"What?" Charlene whispered. "What did you just say?!" She let go of my hand and stared hard at my face.

"I said I'm staying all right."

Charlene just shook her head and began to walk away, straight into the back.

"Wait!" I shouted.

"Why are you going to stay, Luce? What's so goddamn important here?"

I took a deep breath and stared hard into her shiny brown eyes. "Well, you, for starts." I frowned. "You're worth staying for, for sure."

Charlene sighed and looked down at her precious little feet. "Luce, I love you with all my heart. But you need to leave. You need to leave right now. If you can't do it for yourself, do it for me."

Then she moved right beside me and kissed my cheek and turned away, starting to cry all over again.

"Goodbye," she mumbled, and ran away, disappearing behind the double silver doors to the back.

I shook my head and walked on out of the diner, starting to cry myself. I walked on back toward the hotel, and just as I got to the porch I felt a hunk of dirt smack the back of my head. It crumbled apart and fell down the back of my blue shirt mingling with the sweat on my back. I turned around and swore and tried to catch sight of who had thrown it, but there was no one around. Then, as I turned around again, another mound of dirt hit the back of my head, this time loaded down with a rock, and it made me lose my footing and I nearly slipped off the porch, but I grabbed the wooden railing and spun around and ran right for the dirty green bushes out front just as three or four lousy little kids shouted and took off, dropping hunks of dirt. I ran right after them and grabbed the slowest one and shook him so hard his lousy little red baseball cap flew off, and then I froze, I froze right where I stood.

Monte Slates.

"Monte . . ." I mumbled, feeling like crying right there. "Why, fella, why?"

"Eye for an eye, that's what the Bible says."

I held his arm tight, shaking my head.

"What did I do to you, pal? How did I wrong you?"

"Burned my dad's hand." He frowned. "Ran that little baby down, too."

"Do you believe that's all right? Throwing dirt at your own friends like that?"

"I figure if you're a killer, you ain't my friend. I figure if you're a killer and done take a life, you ought to be killed yourself."

"What about being forgiven and all that? What's the Good Book say about that?"

"Not much I can remember. They hung up Jesus and nailed his hands to the cross and he didn't do a thing. You kill somebody yourself, you deserve worse, I figure."

There was nothing for me to say. I couldn't argue with him. I turned him loose and watched him run away, still scared as hell, holding his hand where I had grabbed him.

I walked on over to see Junior at work, but the Gas-N-Go was closed. That's what the sign in the door said anyway. The big movable letter sign out front was empty. Clean and empty. Everything seemed wrong. I knocked on the gray glass once and saw Junior moving around inside. He came to the door and unlocked it and let me in. Junior's big round face was covered in sweat. He was scared as hell. I could nearly see his big red heart beating right out of his big-barreled chest. His eyes were tiny and sharp. He looked ready to cry.

"How you doing, pal?" I asked.

"I've been better," he mumbled.

I patted his shoulder and tried to smile. Clutch was standing behind the counter. I smiled and stared at his gray, wrinkly face. It was a face that belonged in a church. It was the face of some old and benevolent saint or king.

"I guess you come here to tell me you're both quitting."

"What if we intend to stay?" I asked.

Clutch stared at me and smiled. "I'd say I was awful proud of you."

Junior stared at the windows, mumbling to himself. I stood beside him and frowned.

"Listen, Junior, if you aren't sure . . . if you think we should leave . . ."

"No, it's not that." He frowned, shaking his big round head. "It's just, I don't know how wrong those folks are for wanting us to leave."

"Christ Jesus, I know what you mean," I whispered. "That's the thing I can't make right. I mean, I know it ain't right for them to come after us like that, but . . . all the things they said, we did. I can't change any of them now, but I wish . . . I wish I could take it all back."

Clutch patted me on the shoulder, shaking his head.

"If it's meant to be, it's a thing you can't change, Luce."

"How's that?" I asked.

"Maybe all these things happened for a reason. Maybe none of these things were a mistake at all."

"You're telling me you believe it wasn't no mistake I ran that poor baby down?"

"No. I didn't say that. But the Lord works in the strangest of ways. Maybe you're not supposed to see it all as a mistake. Maybe you need to take something from it, something to save yourself. The way I see it, anyway, one life lost is better than two."

I became still and silent and felt everything moving right through me. Then that hollow blue telephone rang. Clutch picked it up and after a few seconds handed it to me.

It was Charlene.

"I'm at the bus depot. I'm leaving town. I want you to come with me."

"But—"

"If you ever want to see me again, my bus leaves at four o'clock. I'll be waiting here until then."

"But—"

That sweet woman hung up and I felt all the emptiness of the world fall upon my tongue.

"Who was that?" Junior asked.

"Charlene," I mumbled.

"What is it?"

"She's leaving town. She wants me to go."

I made it the half-mile to the bus depot in a few minutes and found her sitting there in those lousy blue plastic chairs, holding a single brown suitcase upon her lap, crying there all alone to herself. Oh, my Charlene. Her curly brown hair was hanging in her face. She still had on her lousy Starlite Diner waitress uniform. Her legs were folded underneath her. She looked so delicate and small. I felt my heart breaking right in my chest. She looked up at me and tried to wipe the tears out of her eyes, but then she stopped trying to fight it and began crying some more, lowering her head.

"Jesus, Charlene, what are you doing to me?"

"To you?" she shouted. "To you? Luce, what are you doing to *me?*"

"Well, hell, you just can't pick up and leave like this."

"That's exactly what I'm doing. I'm not gonna stay in town and watch you get yourself hurt on account of me. So either you come with me now or never see me again."

"Christ, Charlene, what about your folks?"

"I left them a note and told them I'd call them from L.A."

"L.A.? You can't go out there alone."

"I was hoping you would come with me."

"But . . . I . . . I can't."

"Why not? There's nothing else here for you. You don't have any family in town anymore. You don't care about your parole. I'm sure you can convince Junior to leave. Why would you stay by yourself?"

"I gotta stay. Or else I'll be running away from this the rest of my life."

"If I tell you I'll love you forever, will you come with me?" she asked, kissing my neck so gently, so sweetly. "If I tell you everything you want to hear right now, will you just get on this bus with me?"

All the words I had ever wanted to say slipped right away.

There was nothing I could think to tell her that would make her understand it all in a different way.

"Charlene . . ." I tried to mumble.

That sweet girl nodded and shook her head. "I know. You already said it. You can't."

"It isn't you, darling. I need to do this for me. Don't you see how it ate up Junior running away his whole life? Don't you see what's been done to his life because of some crime he's been serving every day? I can't run away or it'll just follow me."

I unclasped her hand and kissed her pearly fingertips.

"There's no doubt in my mind we'll be together again," I said. "It's a thing I know in my heart."

"That's a real nice thing to say while I'll be worrying like a fool over you."

"I'm just asking you to give me some time," I said.

"But I can't stay here," she said.

"OK. Then send me the sweetest kiss over the lines as soon as you get to L.A." I tried to smile.

"I love you." She blushed. "I really do. I ought to have made you leave with me sooner. I was just afraid you hadn't forgiven me for letting you down with the baby and all." She kissed my hands and then held me tight. "But this thing between us is true. I can feel it beating there right in your heart. That's why I love you. I love you because you weren't afraid to fall in love with me. I don't want to hear you say anything back because then it'll sound like a lie and I know how you feel now anyway."

I kissed her as hard as I dared and turned away without one other word. Then I was a full block away and I could hear the bus doors close and the brakes become undone and the wheels begin to pull away. I opened my lips and said a few single words that took on the weight of the whole cruel world.

"Goodbye, Charlene Dulaire."

Then I turned and began walking back into town.

It was just beginning to get dark.

I walked out down La Harpie Road, way down off the side of the road. I skittered across any intersections and back toward the Gas-N-Go.

Junior was out front with a tiny brown bag full of plastic letters. He was carrying the ladder toward the big sign out front, then stopped when he saw me coming.

"I'm shaky as hell, Luce. You hold the ladder."

I nodded and took it, watching him climb up awkwardly.

"What are you gonna write?" I asked.

"I don't know yet."

He opened up the bag and took out two rounded black letters: a *T* and an *O*.

"Hey, let me ask you something," I said. "It's something I've wanted to know for a while anyways."

"OK," he mumbled, still trying to eat.

"What the hell is your first name anyway?"

"My name?" He smiled.

"Sure, sure, it ain't Junior, is it?"

"No." He smiled. "It ain't. It's Ervis. Ervis Breen."

"Ervis!" I smiled. "What kind of name is that?"

"Family name, I guess. I guess I'm named after someone or another. Never did like it much myself. My dad was the one who took to calling me Junior instead. Serves me better, I think."

"Makes you sound like you're a gas station attendant all right. Could have been a rocket scientist or lawyer with a name like Ervis, I bet."

"It might have all been a little different then."

The dull white moon came up and hung right over our heads. It made me wonder where my Charlene was. Riding on some bus, all alone, somewhere along some highway right now, somewhere close, somewhere far away. Nestled between some elderly lady and an overweight traveling salesman, she was safe at least. I looked up and watched Junior sorting through the letters, mumbling little words to himself. He began the next word, starting with an *F*, as a light flashed upon us.

A car passed down the road, shining its headlights through the dark. Then it stopped. It stopped and slowly began to back up. Junior dropped the bag of silent words and hurried down the ladder, panicked.

"I'm scared, Luce. I'm scared as hell."

"I'm scared, too, pal."

"Whatever happens, Luce, I want you to know you're the best friend I ever had."

The car, a Chevy, turned around in the middle of the road and began to slowly head our way. I looked at Junior, then whispered, "OK, pal, start running." I held my breath and started off, my feet hitting the dirt as fast as they could. I heard Junior behind me crying, but I never stopped to turn around and look.

tonight

We hurried down the side of the road, sneaking along the culvert to the woods, where we waited by the river, doing our best to catch our breath.

Everything was still and all the stars in the heavens above began to spin around, pinning us right down in place. Some mockingbirds chirped some quiet regretful tunes, flickering their wings in the dark. Tiny white insects darted on by, shimmering like felled constellations. We could hear strange voices and saw the flash of headlights just beyond the edge of the heavy green trees. We crept to the small gray boathouse, the same one I had first been to with Charlene, and there I found the rowboat.

"We can head down river awhile, then cut back to town," I said. Junior hauled the small boat in his arms, placing it in the trembling water. We climbed inside, holding our breath as the river immediately pulled us along.

There was a warm-eyed fawn resting its little brown eyes over the river's edge. It disappeared right back into the dark as soon as the rowboat approached. Beneath us in the murky depths, a twelve-point buck lay still and lit up by a thousand stars stuck in its antlers. Everything turned dark and strange. A spooky old hoot owl crooned and muffled up its breast as we swung on past, crashing into thick green branches and cattails, drifting farther and farther away, deeper and deeper downstream. We were trapped. Trapped beneath all of creation, beneath all the things that had judged us and our sins and all the strange and horrible things we'd already seen and done.

We spun on down that river, plummeting along, crashing into reeds and upturned rocks, Junior silent, his head rolling heavily on his big shoulders.

"*Perdition*," Junior whispered. "We're heading straight down."

I shook my head.

"We're heading straight down to darkness," Junior whimpered. "Straight to the Devil hisself."

I could hear things chattering and whispering out in the dark as the rowboat caught hold of a current and began to spin straight into a gruesome patch of gray-silver rocks. The boat pounded hard against the slate, loosening its boards along the bow. Then it all broke loose. The boat began to fall apart right under our weight.

"We're doomed," Junior cried. "Doomed to an eternity in hopeless hell." Water began to fill up the boat around Junior's feet. His hefty weight was pulling us right on down.

"Hush up now," I mumbled. "Just be still." The boat was sinking. The cold gray water began to rise up to my chest as I kicked free. I dug one arm under Junior's neck and pulled us both out of the boat, just its nose rising out of the wake, still drifting, floating off and away down the river and straight into the dark of the night. Junior was as heavy as a tombstone. He felt like he was made of stiff and solid rocks. I pulled and breathed hard with all my guts and finally towed him up into the high mass of thin yellow grass.

I lay there in that cold water for a long time. I lay there on the bank the rest of the night until I felt the first rays of sunlight beam down upon my face.

Then I opened my eyes.

Then I pulled myself up on the grass all the way. I looked down to see if Junior was awake. He stared back at me with his big eyes and flopped beside me on the bank. He dropped his face in the dirt and began crying, digging his big fingers in the mud.

"Get up," I whispered, wiping my mouth. "Come on now, get up."

"I can't," he muttered, keeping his face against the ground. "I can't go on no more."

"Listen to me, Junior. You're gonna get the hell up and we're gonna tread back into town and down to the bus depot and get out of here all right. Now get up, man. Get up right now so we can leave once and for all."

"No," he mumbled. "You go on. Just leave me. Leave me here so they can finish me off."

I grabbed hold of the back of his shirt and shook him hard.

"Get up!!" I shouted. "Right now!! Get up and move!!" I kept tugging on his shirt and his big head, pulling him up. He struggled to his feet and wiped some of the dirt off his chin and leaned against me, still crying, still muttering to himself.

"Now we're gonna walk, you hear? We're gonna walk right to the bus depot and get the hell out, OK?"

He nodded once and we started walking, edging along the woods down a thin brown path. We were both silent. Junior's eyes were all gray. He looked strangely peaceful, peaceful and quiet and accepting as all hell. My own face was a twisted-up portrait of rage. My bad eye had swelled up again. We tracked back toward La Harpie through the woods, cutting across some farms to avoid being seen. The sun was up and reaching its height, and right from town I could hear church bells beginning to ring. Everything under my feet was dull and brown and dirty. Junior's face was still calm. He walked beside me, staring straight ahead, silent as ever, watching the horizon as it grew from behind rows and rows of stiff yellow corn. We made it out to La Harpie Road, about a half-mile from town, a half-mile from the bus, and then in the middle of someone's cornfield, still as could be in that morning light, Junior stopped and stared down at his hands like he had just taken the last step he might ever take.

"Wait," he mumbled. "Oh, Jesus, just wait."

"What is it?" I asked.

"I need to go back. I need to go to the hotel."

"The hotel? What the hell are you talking about?"

His big round face shined with grease.

"I need that photograph. I need to get it back."

"Photograph?"

"My photograph."

"Dammit, Junior. You go back there, those men are going to kill you. It's just a goddamn picture. You have to let it go."

"I can't. I can't."

His big blue eyes shined deeply.

"Jesus, pal, can't you get another goddamn picture some-where else?"

"No," he muttered. "This is the only one. The only one."

"Jesus." I shook my head.

"She's dead, Luce. Dead and gone."

"I know."

"No, you don't. She's dead. By my own hand. I sent her down a river on a raft."

"Christ," I whispered. I felt like I was about to vomit. The sun began to spin above my head. Everything else faded to red.

"She was fourteen years old and got pregnant from the man down the road. He had a wife and two kids and she kept being pregnant a secret. I did what I thought would save her."

"Christ Jesus. Jesus."

"I put her out of reach. I took those two lives to keep her pure. Now I only got one to give back to her."

"No, no, Junior. Don't think like that. We have to leave town. Right now. We can't go back."

"That's all I have left. That's the only sign that she ever was. That photograph. I need to go get it and then I'll meet you at the bus depot."

"Junior, don't. Junior, no!!" But he was already down the road, limping along. I watched his thick form cross the road into town and disappear behind a line of trees. I stood there for a minute more. I don't know. I guess I was waiting for him to turn around, to turn back, but he didn't. He just disappeared right behind those thick green elm trees and faded right away.

I turned and began walking fast. The sun was beginning to peak and it was hot as hell on my back. No one was around. No cars passed. Most of the entire town was at church right about now. My face felt sore. My teeth began to chatter again. I took a deep breath to try to keep myself together and took a step ahead.

I made it to the bus depot and bought myself a ticket from a man with a long thin mustache. He stared at me for a long moment as if considering whether he should sell me the ticket or not. I sat down and waited. Two minutes went by. Then something spurred me beneath my skin. I was sure Junior had run into trouble. I ran right out of the depot and back into town, right past the gray town hall and the little antique shop and the church steps and the bingo hall. I didn't care who saw me now. I wanted to die or be sure Junior was OK. The church bells began to ring hard in my ears. They burned deep in my brain with solemn golden tones as I turned and headed toward the hotel.

I ran down the street holding my breath, sure any sound I made would tell the whole town where I was. I made it a block away from the hotel and looked around. The street was empty. I kept my breath in and walked quickly toward the hotel, toward the front porch. It was all quiet and faded white.

A shot rang out.

BOOM!!!

I ran the rest of the way down the block and pulled the front door open hard and ran down the hall to the front stairs and started up, feeling my whole head fill with blood. Someone passed me on the stairs, some tenant whose face was unlit and dark and headed on their way down. I was on the second-floor landing, then up on the third floor and down the hall, and then there it was, his open door, wide and parted, a kind of perfectly rectangular dark space. Less than a minute had gone by. Less than a minute had burned out. I stared at that blank open doorway. Some light poured on out. Some dust hung about, dancing like tiny angels in the wake. I ran right inside and caught sight of his big gray body gathered in a lump on his belly on the floor. His head laid right against the closet door. His sideburns looked thick and gray and covered in sweat. His big left hand was outstretched and reaching ahead. The other was draped beside his round white cheek.

There was his blood spread across the room. Cold and silent and still.

There were two small words left beside his chubby white face, spelled out in perfect red letters left by his tender white digits, still and perfect beside where his right hand was laid.

"to forgive"

That was it. All he could say. Written perfectly in his own blood. Written perfectly and left for no one to see.

It was all done. It was all gone.

There was a halo of maroon that rose from the back of his head. He had been shot with his back turned by some unknown man, a coward, a man who didn't even have the courage to stare poor Junior in the face.

I was trembling. I was falling down. I was holding the wall to stand up as Old Lady St. Francis came running up the stairs. I began to back away and run down the stairs and out the door just as that old woman's scream filled my ears.

I ran fast as I could down to the middle of town, following the church bells until I was standing on the chapel steps. I put my hand to the big gold handle and then stopped myself. I could hear the organist's soft-keyed hymn and that town's lowly golden song. Then the church went still. Everyone was quiet, listening to the words coming from the pulpit.

A good man, I thought to myself, standing on the steps. *A very penitent man must have shot him in the head.*

I turned from that church and walked on out and waited for a single shot to knock me out of my body and down the cold white stone steps of the chapel. But it never came. The organist's hymn resumed, and the congregation all took voice in a low, sullen kind of tune, singing softly as I limped down the street, keeping my eyes nearly closed, still waiting, still waiting for that single shot to the back of my head. I made it all the way to the bus depot and sat there in a dirty blue seat. No one came after me.

G-U-I-L-T-Y

I carved that word in the blue plastic bus depot seat with my old room key so someone might see. When the bus pulled up, I took my seat on board and waited again. Everything seemed ready to fall apart. Everything seemed thin and frail and weak.

Then the bus door swung closed suddenly with a hush. And all at once, everything disappeared. There was no sound. There was no movement. There was nothing behind me now. There was only somewhere to go. Someplace to leave.

I settled into that empty red seat and stared out the window as the bus began to roll forward and the world rolled past.

Junior Breen was dead. It was written there in the lines upon my hands. Upon my own face. I leaned back in the seat. I laid my head against the window and began to cry.

There was no voice or word sent from him to see me off. But he was close. Everything I had ever held to me was now close. I began to cry some more and hold my face in my shirtsleeve. It was covered with dirt and blood and mud. It was full of the heavy musk of water and sweat and dirt.

I cleared the tears out of my eyes and stared hard out the window.

Somewhere out there the truth was waiting. Somewhere out there, something had to be waiting for me. With my poor Charlene. It seemed like she was the only thing I could still imagine. The only thing I could still see as real.

Later, riding through the dark, crying to myself, alone on that bus, I thought about everything, about Charlene and the gas station and poor ol' Junior and Clutch and Monte and L.B. and Old Lady St. Francis and all the other things I had tried to keep from myself. All the guilt and pity and shame that stretched out behind me dark as the road ahead. There was nothing out there but the blue-and-red-and-white spade-shaped sign that read *"Interstate 80"* and the low hum of the big silver wheels flying over the pavement, the quiet rumble of the engine and bus as it passed over another mile of blackness, slipping down along the thin yellow lines that divided the road from the twilight, and the night from the road below. There all alone I realized something. Maybe Charlene and I were already together. Maybe I was already beside her. There was the night right between us. It moved from me to her in silent black waves, whispering all the things I had been afraid to say. There was the darkness, and we had shared that together, too. Now there was nothing between us but space and time—space which fell silent under the quiet breath of the dark sky, and time that disappeared beneath the restraint of the black rubber wheels. There was nothing behind us now but the black-ness in our dreams and nothing ahead of us either, not yet, there was only us and the hush of the cool blue night, playing on between us like a gentle little lullaby. It all made me wonder. It all made me think.

Junior was dead. He was gone and finally put to rest. But what kind of man deserved to be killed like that? What kind of man had the right to do such a goddamn wicked thing?

I closed my eyes and cried some more.

The darkness had already fallen above me with an answer to it all. It moved over everything, over good and evil, over impure and pious men just the same. Just the same. There was no differ-ence between a saint and sinner in the skin, in the flesh. It all came from the sweet blood within. It all came from the tender truth hidden deep inside. The difference between the two was a thin, wavering gentle line. It might change in the heart with each lulling beat. It might change in the soft time it takes to breathe. I had done my best to be a good man. I had done my best to live a decent life, even if I had fallen short some of the time. I had tried to keep my heart pure and return the love I had felt, and it wasn't until then, when I was on that bus alone, that I thought I might be all right. Maybe it's not a thing that is easy to see or feel. Maybe it isn't exactly clear how your heart beats, good or evil, dishonest or sweet, until it's your time all alone in the dark, listening to the quiet whisper of your own lonely heart, the empty thump of your own fears shivering like an old kettle drum, bent and rusted and warped all wrong, or the distant murmur of all your hope, the lonely lullaby of a hula girl's song.

Also available from Akashic Books

HAIRSTYLES OF THE DAMNED
by Joe Meno
290 pages, a trade paperback original, $13.95, ISBN: 1-888451-70-X
*PUNK PLANET BOOKS, a BARNES & NOBLE DISCOVER PROGRAM selection

"Joe Meno writes with the energy, honesty, and emotional impact of the best punk rock. From the opening sentence to the very last word, *Hairstyles of the Damned* held me in his grip."
—Jim DeRogatis, pop music critic, *Chicago Sun-Times*

CHICAGO NOIR edited by Neal Pollack
300 pages, a trade paperback original, $15.95, ISBN: 1-888451-89-0

Brand new stories by: Joe Meno, Neal Pollack, Achy Obejas, Alexai Galaviz-Budziszewski, Daniel Buckman, Adam Langer, Todd Dills, Peter Orner, Kevin Guilfoile, Bayo Ojikuto, Jeffrey Renard Allen, Claire Zulkey, Andrew Ervin, M.K. Meyers, Luciano Guerriero, C.J. Sullivan, Amy Sayre-Roberts, and Jim Arndorfer.

The hard-bitten streets of Chicago once represented by James Farrell and Nelson Algren have shifted locales, but it is still a place where people struggle to survive and where, for many, crime is the only means for their survival. The stories in *Chicago Noir* reclaim that territory.

LESSONS IN TAXIDERMY
by Bee Lavender
168 pages, a trade paperback original, $12.95, ISBN: 1-888451-79-3
*PUNK PLANET BOOKS

"Lavender . . . holds nothing back as she recounts her life spent in and out of hospitals and her subsequent dissociation from her own body and emotions. She struggles with health problems from birth, which are compounded by her surroundings, including frequent encounters with street fights, domestic violence and poverty. Her voice is as strong as the front she puts up for the multitude of doctors she sees, and it's hard not to be in awe of what one fragile human being can withstand in the course of such a short lifetime . . . witnessing her strength and sheer determination to live makes this striking book completely engrossing."
—*Publishers Weekly* (starred review)

SOUTHLAND by Nina Revoyr
348 pages, a trade paperback original, $15.95, ISBN: 1-888451-41-6
*Winner of a LAMBDA LITERARY AWARD & FERRO-GRUMLEY AWARD
*EDGAR AWARD finalist

"If Oprah still had her book club, this novel likely would be at the top of her list . . . With prose that is beautiful, precise, but never pretentious . . ."

—*Booklist*

"*Southland* merges elements of literature and social history with the propulsive drive of a mystery, while evoking Southern California as a character, a key player in the tale. Such aesthetics have motivated other Southland writers, most notably Walter Mosley."

—*Los Angeles Times*

ADIOS MUCHACHOS by Daniel Chavarría
245 pages, a trade paperback original, $13.95, ISBN: 1-888451-16-5
*Winner of the EDGAR AWARD

"Out of the mystery wrapped in an enigma that, over the last forty years, has been Cuba for the U.S., comes a Uruguayan voice so cheerful, a face so laughing, and a mind so deviously optimistic that we can only hope this is but the beginning of a flood of Latin America's indomitable novelists, playwrights, storytellers. Welcome, Daniel Chavarría."

—Donald Westlake, author of *Trust Me on This*

THE COCAINE CHRONICLES
edited by Gary Phillips & Jervey Tervalon
269 pages, a trade paperback original, $14.95, ISBN: 1-888451-75-0

The best fiction anthology of cocaine-themed tales to blow through in years, featuring seventeen original stories by Susan Straight, Lee Child, Laura Lippman, Ken Bruen, Jerry Stahl, Nina Revoyr, and others.

"*The Cocaine Chronicles* is a pure, jangled hit of urban, gritty, and raw noir. Caution: These stories are addicting."

—Harlan Coben, award-winning author of *Just One Look*